Ian Fleming's James Bond 007 in

DIE ANOTHER DAY

A novel by

Raymond Benson

Based on the screenplay by

Neal Purvis & Robert Wade

BERKLEY BOULEVARD BOOKS, NEW YORK

DIE ANOTHER DAY

A Berkley Boulevard Book / published by arrangement with
Ian Fleming (Glidrose) Publications Ltd.

PRINTING HISTORY
Berkley Boulevard edition / November 2002

Visit our website at
www.penguinputnam.com

ISBN: 0-425-18963-5

BERKLEY BOULEVARD
Berkley Boulevard Books are published by
The Berkley Publishing Group,
a division of Penguin Putnam Inc.,
375 Hudson Street, New York, New York 10014.
BERKLEY BOULEVARD and its logo
are trademarks belonging to Penguin Putnam Inc.

PRINTED IN THE UNITED STATES OF AMERICA

10   9   8   7   6   5   4   3   2   1

Contents

1

Surf's Up

A man could easily die out here.

The thought passed through his head as he and his two companions fought the raging surf, desperately clinging to their boards.

The full moon illuminated the distant coastline with an eerie, white glow that created phantoms out of the concrete pillboxes and radar dishes. The moonlight wasn't adequate for their purposes, but the night-vision goggles made up for the deficit. Through them he could actually see the barbed wire that fortified the beach. The sharp points glistened like stars dotting the landscape.

The three men paddled the surfboards furiously in an attempt to catch a massive wave. They managed to get up, but not for long. The huge wave quickly crashed over and wiped out two of the surfers. The one man who kept his balance found himself on top of what he estimated to be a sixty-footer. If he hadn't been concentrating on the seriousness of the mission, he might have enjoyed it.

Eventually the wave levelled out and the surfer glided elegantly across the dark, silvery water, effortlessly changing direction when he needed to and finally floating silently to the shallows. He stepped off and walked quickly up the sand.

The surfer crouched in the shadows just as a sentry came around the bend. Painfully, he willed himself to slow his breathing so that the guard wouldn't hear him.

As expected, the sentry was dressed in the uniform of the North Korean army. He carried an AK-47 and probably had a handgun attached to a belt. The surfer watched as the sentry noticed the surfboard wash up on the sand. The guard stepped over to it, curious and surprised to find such an object on this isolated and closely watched beach.

The surfer made his move. Like a jungle cat, he sprung out of his hiding place, lightly ran the few feet across the sand, and struck the sentry from behind. The guard collapsed beside the board.

James Bond removed the night-vision goggles and looked up and down the beach. There was no sign of anyone else. He scanned the surf and finally saw his two wet-suited colleagues struggle onto the beach. They ran over to him and removed their own goggles. His enigmatic companions nodded to him. They, too, were breathless and needed to gather their strength for the challenges ahead.

Bond squatted by the surfboard and took hold of the fin. With a click, he twisted it, and a compartment slid out of the edge of the board with a satisfying rasp. Inside was everything he needed: his Walther P99 and several magazines of ammunition, nylon rope, a tray of C4 plastic explosive, and a combat knife with a Global Positioning System device built into its handle.

He stood and surveyed the beach again. The radar dish on the dunes behind them would suit their very precise needs. The two surfers read his mind and ran up the beach towards it as Bond unzipped his wet suit. He pulled it off, revealing a smart Brioni suit. The shoes were hidden in the surfboard. By the time he was dressed for the role he was about to play, the two Koreans from the South who had ridden the waves beside him had also shed their wet suits, revealing North Korean army uniforms.

The mission to Pukch'ong Beach was extremely dangerous. Everyone knew it. Even M had given Bond a chance to let someone else do it, but 007 had looked back at her with fearless self-assurance. The risks and the high stakes of a meticulously planned—and brilliantly executed—military raid remained Bond's first love. There was no question but that he would go through with it. As for the two South Koreans, they shared Bond's grim purpose and dedication to the job at hand. Don and Lee. Bond didn't know their last names and didn't want to know. They seemed capable enough, but it was always a good idea not to become too friendly with fellow operatives. You never knew when someone might not return.

Don used his blade to sever a power cable attached to the radar dish while Lee took Bond's combat knife and thrust it into the ground. The handle automatically split open to form a small dish—the GPS beacon device that was one of Q Branch's more ingenious inventions.

Within seconds, they could hear a faintly audible signal.

Some sixty miles away, a Russian-made Kamov Ka-26 Hoodlum helicopter flew over the dense forest that made up much of the North Korean peninsula. The North Korean army pilot noticed that a new indicator had lit up on the beacon interrogator screen that pulsed in front of him. The flight system recalibrated to direct the helicopter towards the new landing zone. The pilot made a slight adjustment in his heading, then turned to look back at his passenger.

The man had been clutching a briefcase to his chest ever since he had boarded the chopper. He seemed to be extremely nervous.

The pilot turned back, chuckling to himself. Westerners were either cowards or idiots, and this one seemed to be both.

As the Hoodlum made a subtle change in direction, a sliver of sun peered over the horizon and broke the night sky into thousands of warm colours.

Ten minutes later, James Bond and his two companions heard the approaching helicopter. The Koreans took their positions on the sand and stood to attention as the Hoodlum appeared over the hills behind the beach, circled, and hovered tentatively. The pilot was naturally cautious, as the landing zone differed from the original plan. Finally, the helicopter gently descended and set down on the sand. The rotors slowed as the pilot unbuckled his seat belt, opened the door, and hopped out. He looked over at the two soldiers. They saluted. The pilot halfheartedly returned the salute and then turned to help the passenger out. The man was still clutching the case as if it held his life-support system.

When the new arrivals turned back around, they saw

that the two Korean soldiers had drawn their weapons and a third man had joined them. James Bond stood between them, Walther in hand and a pleasant grin on his face. The man holding the case was surprised, for he thought he was looking into a mirror. He was dressed in exactly the same style of suit as Bond. The pilot and passenger slowly raised their hands.

Bond stepped forward and took the passenger's brief-case. The two Koreans worked quickly. They tied and gagged the pilot and passenger and marched them over behind the radar dish. Another few loops of the ropes secured the two prisoners safely out of sight, ensuring that they wouldn't be discovered for several hours. Too late.

Bond and the two Koreans boarded the Hoodlum and buckled in. Don sat at the controls, made some adjustments, then guided the chopper into the air.

Bond set the case on his lap and opened it. It was full of sparkling, dazzling diamonds. Lee glanced over at it and couldn't help but gasp in awe. Bond removed the C4 from a packet and carefully pressed the substance under the bottom lining in the case. The detonator was the size of a cigarette, and this he plunged into the explosive. The remote was next, which he wired to the detonator. He then activated a switch on the edge of his Omega wristwatch. The remote beeped.

Bond looked at Lee, who nodded. Bond shut the case, settled back for the ride south to Colonel Moon's compound, and reflected on what he was about to do.

North Korea was arguably the most dangerous place on earth for a captured spy. The Democratic People's Republic of Korea refused to allow even genuine journalists into the country, much less anyone who could possibly be an agent of either South Korea or the despised countries of the West. Intelligence-service lore was filled with horrific yet hauntingly unsubstantiated tales of what had happened to agents caught north of the 38th Parallel. Bond and his companions could certainly expect torture followed by death if they were unmasked.

Increasingly isolated even from the Communist world, North Korea was a mysterious land about which reliable intelligence was sparse. A bitter civil war had ended with the peninsula's division into two hostile parts half a century ago. Kim Il Sung ruled North Korea unopposed. Now there were rumours of mass famine, of rival factions vying for power, rumours that Kim Jong Il, the country's current leader, was a mere puppet controlled by a secret cabal of generals. Foreign intelligence sources were convinced that the DPRK was developing nuclear, biological, and chemical weapons. North Korea refused steadfastly to allow inspectors into the country to confirm or refute these allegations. Even her staunchest allies, the Chinese, had begun to treat North Korea with suspicion.

Tensions around the Demilitarized Zone north of the 38th Parallel remained as high as they'd been at the end of the Korean War; to this day, North Koreans call that conflict the "Fatherland Liberation War." According to their history books, South Korea, aided by the Americans and British Commonwealth countries, had attacked the peaceful North Koreans, who repelled them with sticks and rocks, driving them back into the southern part of the Korean peninsula, from which they might at any moment launch a new attack on the northern "socialist paradise."

6

Two South Korean agents had lost their lives un-earthing valuable information on a young hard-liner by the name of Moon who had created a loyal semiprivate army that supported his aggressive stance against South Korea and the West. It was believed that Moon was financing his operations with the sale of illegal diamonds from the warring nations in Africa—so-called conflict diamonds. Colonel Moon was considered to be highly dangerous, perhaps the most corrupt and volatile man in the North Korean army. He was a rogue element who could start a war overnight. It had become inescapable logic that he had to be eliminated. This situation was made complicated and more delicate by the fact that Moon was the son of one of the army's more moderate generals—a man with good intentions with regard to a unified Korea.

It had been a rough night. Once the requisite intelligence regarding the exchange of diamonds had been received, Bond and his two Korean cohorts had only had three hours to launch the mission. Bond had been in a holding pattern in South Korea for over a week, waiting for the green light. Finally, just after 02:00 in the morning, the word came through. Van Bierk, the diamond trader, was on the way to meet Moon. As Van Bierk was white, had dark hair and blue eyes, and was roughly Bond's size, M had made 007 the prime candidate for the job. Don and Lee had been recruited from South Korea's elite Special Forces unit—officially off the record—that specialised in counterterrorism and clandestine military activity. The three men had been flown with their gear at low altitude in an army helicopter from Yanggu, over Tongjosŏn Bay, to a point three miles offshore from Pukch'ong's nearby beach.

They were dropped into the choppy water with their surfboards and now they were ready to execute the second phase of the mission.

The sweat rolled off Colonel Tan-Gun Moon's bare torso as he struck the punching bag repeatedly. It hung heavily from the ceiling in the makeshift gym, sparsely decorated in typical Korean style. Colonel Moon liked to begin each day with a strenuous workout. He was extremely fit, and he intended to stay that way. The future leader of a united Korea needed to be a strong and powerful man. At twenty-seven years of age and the handsome son of a respected army general, Moon believed it to be his destiny to rule his country.

An officer stood nearby, watching Moon pummel the punching bag until the colonel had finished and turned away.

"Let him out," he ordered the officer in his native tongue.

The officer stepped forward and unzipped the punching bag. An unconscious man, bruised and bloody, spilled out onto the floor.

Moon looked back at the pile of flesh and said, "That will teach you to lecture me." The slow sound of a helicopter making its descent caught Moon's attention. He grabbed a towel and wiped the sweat from his body before putting on his military tunic. He then reached for his colonel's hat, which sat on a bronze bust of his head. Moon motioned to the officer, who bent down to drag the beaten man away.

"Find me a new anger therapist!" Moon barked, then he went out of the room in the opposite direction.

The compound was located on a hill overlooking the

Demilitarized Zone on the north side of the 38th Parallel. Moon liked to call it a villa, even though it was really a glorified bunker, a border gunpost that was the lair of a true warlord. The walls were made of solid concrete, fortified with pillboxes and barbed wire. Sentries lined every visible portion that faced the south. They were always ready for any possible attack, however unlikely. The Demilitarized Zone was a no-man's-land full of mines, booby traps, death, and destruction. Only a fool would dare to venture into it.

Colonel Moon's compound wasn't large, but it was certainly unique. Just beyond the fortified walls was a courtyard with enough space for a helipad and several military vehicles. At one side of the courtyard was a collection of half a dozen luxury sports cars, including a Jaguar XKR, a Ferrari, and a Lamborghini.

As the Hoodlum helicopter descended into the courtyard, a man dressed unobtrusively in civilian clothes stood aside and waited. Many of the soldiers stationed at the bunker called him "the Man Who Never Smiles," but not to his face. Indeed, this man, who seemed to follow the colonel everywhere, was a mysterious cipher who maintained a deadpan expression at all times. Even now, as he watched the helicopter land, his eyes betrayed no emotion.

James Bond opened the door of the helicopter and stepped onto the tarmac. The briefcase was in his hand.

The civilian surreptitiously aimed a small Sony Ericsson PDA at him, capturing his image with a built-in CMOS camera. The man pressed a button and the word SEND flashed over Bond's picture on the tiny screen.

As Bond looked over and saw him, the man pocketed the PDA and walked forward.

"I am Zao," he said in English. "You are late."

"I had to tie up a few loose ends," Bond said.

Zao turned to the back of the courtyard just as Colonel Moon, now dressed in full military uniform, emerged. His eyes never left Bond's face as he walked towards him. As he passed his retinue of guards and soldiers, each man visibly cowered.

"Mr. Van Bierk," he said in fluent, cultured English. "I've been looking forward to this meeting."

"Me, too," Bond replied, offering his hand. Moon ignored it. "My, um, African military friends owe you many thanks. Few men have the guts to trade African conflict diamonds since the UN embargo."

Colonel Moon gave a thin, sour smile. "I know all about the UN. I studied at Oxford and Harvard. I majored in Western hypocrisy."

Bond raised his eyebrows and gestured. "From your modest little car collection, I'd never have guessed."

Moon snapped, "Show me the diamonds."

"Show *me* the weapons." There was no mistaking the obduracy behind these words.

The colonel studied Bond. Few men had ever shown such toughness with him. None dared do so now. Moon immediately knew that he had met a hard man of unusual strength and determination. He looked at Zao and nodded curtly. Zao spoke into a walkie-talkie, and immediately the distant roar of engines attracted Bond's attention to the Demilitarized Zone.

A concrete block at the gate began to rise, and Bond could see lights swimming in the clouds of dust, growing larger, coming closer.

Trucks? Impossible! Bond thought.

"Hiding weapons in the Demilitarized Zone?" he

10

asked Moon. "Very stylish, Colonel. That's a bit of a minefield out there."

Moon replied sardonically, "America's cultural contribution to our country. One million land mines." Moon's voice could not conceal his pride as he declared, "And my hovercraft float right over them."

Bond turned back to look through the gates. The man was right. The vehicles were indeed hovercraft. One was a huge military carrier, a mothership that was a magnificent piece of machinery. Four smaller hovercraft accompanied it, gliding like wraiths over the vast, mine-pitted wasteland bordered by skull-and-crossbones signs. Hovercraft have the ability to fly a few inches off the ground on a cushion of air and are lifted by the thrust of fans ducted through double-skin hulls. The lift air is contained under the craft by flexible segmented skirts that keep the air cushion pressure up. Bond knew that hovercraft do not set off mines over which they travel because they produce virtually no acoustic, magnetic, or pressure signatures.

The mothership flew into the compound, slowed and settled to the ground. The four smaller hovercraft came to rest alongside it, two on each side. Bond could see that the larger ship was bristling with an abundance of weaponry and matériel: machine guns, ammunition, mortars, flamethrowers, land mines, bulletproof vests, and a variety of small arms. Deep drawers slid out of the flanks, revealing even more weapons inside.

"RPGs, flamethrowers, automatic weapons, and enough ammunition to run a small war," Moon said proudly. Then he smiled for the first time. "The diamonds?"

Bond presented the case to him. Moon took it and

handed it to a bespectacled man standing behind him. The man opened it and showed the sparkling interior to Moon.

"Don't blow it all at once," Bond said.

"Oh, I have special plans for this consignment," Moon replied.

The bespectacled man took the case to a table, pulled out an eyepiece, and began to examine the loot. Bond was disappointed that Moon didn't take the explosives-laden case himself, but he was careful not to show it.

A mobile phone rang. The man called Zao reached into his pocket and answered it. He slipped on an earpiece, then took out the PDA camera. A large red *X* blinked over Bond's image.

Bond sensed that something was terribly wrong. When Zao looked up at him with narrow, lizard-like eyes, he was sure of it.

Zao approached the colonel and whispered in his ear.

Moon smiled again and addressed Bond. "Let me show you our new Tank Buster."

He reached over the side of the mothership and grabbed a heavy combination grenade launcher/machine gun.

"Depleted uranium shells, naturally," he said.

"Naturally," Bond said, slightly uneasy.

Moon considered his choice of targets within the terrain. Then, without warning, he swung it around and pointed it at the Hoodlum helicopter, where Don and Lee still sat. Before Bond could react, Moon let rip. A massive grenade shot through the chopper, which exploded with a deafening blast.

In the same instant Zao drew a handgun and pointed

it at Bond's head. Bond had no choice but to raise his hands.

Through the black smoke, one of the South Koreans came running out, his body aflame. Colonel Moon flipped the Tank Buster, aimed the machine-gun portion at the poor man, and, with a single shot, took him out.

"Amazing accuracy," Moon commented, impressed with the weapon. He turned to Bond. "So you are James Bond, a British assassin. And how do you propose to kill me now, Mr. Bond?"

Bond froze. How did they know his name? And how was he going to get out of this fix?

2

Shooting Gallery

There was still a chance.

As Moon stepped towards the briefcase on the table, Bond reached for the trigger button on his watch.

"Don't move!" Zao commanded as he forced Bond's arms apart and began to pat him down. He found the Walther and removed it.

Moon came back to Bond and spoke into his face. "It is pathetic that you British still believe you have the right—no, the duty—to police the world. You're as redundant as those mines out there will soon become." He paused to regain his composure and then said, "But you won't live to see the day all Korea is ruled by the North."

Bond replied, "Then you and I have something in common."

Moon smirked and moved near the diamonds again.

Bond decided then and there to sacrifice himself for the mission. He would blow up the case and take everyone with him. The explosion wouldn't be huge—he might even survive. Bond moved his hands closer together, ready to detonate the bomb—but then Zao's walkie-talkie buzzed. The henchman answered it and his normally unemotional face grew concerned. He handed the receiver to Moon and said in Korean, "It's the general."

Bond's command of the Korean language was weak, at best. But he knew enough to catch the gist of what was being said.

Moon spoke into the walkie-talkie, obviously shocked. "Father?" He listened for a moment, stiffened, then shut it off. He looked at Zao and said, "He's five minutes away. He heard the explosion and wants to know what's going on." He shook his head and began to stride away. Over his shoulder, he shouted an order to everyone standing nearby, "Get the weapons out of here!"

He stopped, as if he had forgotten something, and turned to Zao. "Kill the spy." Bond had no trouble understanding that.

Zao nodded and stood beside the diamonds as Moon climbed aboard the mothership. Moon shouted to the driver, and in seconds the hovercraft lifted and moved off, followed by two of the smaller craft.

Zao drew his pistol and pointed it at Bond, but at the same instant Bond hit the button on his watch.

The briefcase exploded just feet away from Zao and covered the henchman with diamond shrapnel. Bond dropped and rolled as Zao's bullet shot over his head. Zao fell to the ground as Bond leapt up and ran after Moon's convoy.

Zao lifted his head. His face was lacerated and pitted with glittering matter. Despite the pain, he scanned the courtyard and saw Bond running towards one of the two remaining small hovercraft. He pulled himself off the ground and staggered to the Jaguar XKR, the nearest of Moon's valuable cars. He leaned in through the open window and punched a button on the dashboard. A machine gun appeared and rose from a compartment in the rear. Zao took hold of it, trained it on Bond, and began strafing the courtyard with bullets, trailing destruction just inches behind the enemy spy. As he was half-blinded by the wounds on his face, Zao's hail of bullets was wildly inaccurate but still dangerous. Some of the bullets had punctured the petrol tanks in several of Moon's fancy cars, causing a domino effect of explosions down the line. The British agent avoided the gunfire and jumped onto the fighter escort hovercraft as it was taking off.

The gunner on the back of the hovercraft couldn't believe his eyes as Bond rolled onto the deck of the moving vehicle. He turned his gun to blast him, but Bond deftly grabbed the barrel and swung it around into the gunner's face, knocking him out.

Back in the courtyard, Zao yelled to the crew of the remaining hovercraft, ordering them to give pursuit.

Bond looked back and saw that the fourth hovercraft was taking off. His own craft was just passing through the arch at the compound gate. Thinking quickly, he angled the rear gun at the control mechanism mounted on the gate and fired. Bond's craft zipped through the opening just as the huge keystone fell with an earth-shaking thud. The driver of the pursuing hovercraft had no time to stop and slammed straight into it. The explosion rocked the compound.

As Bond's craft sailed into the Demilitarized Zone, he moved forward and grabbed the pilot by the neck. He pulled the man away from the controls and threw him over the side. The man fell directly onto a mine in the dirt and disappeared in a fireball. Bond was now in command of the hovercraft.

Up ahead, Colonel Moon had witnessed what the British spy had done and was intrigued and excited by the man's fortitude. At last, here was an adversary worth fighting! He was obviously not like other Westerners. It would be a pleasure to defeat him.

Moon picked up the Tank Buster and shot at the ground behind him, setting off mines in front of Bond's hovercraft. Bond was gaining on the two escort craft just as the explosions jolted his vehicle with showers of rock and soil. He lunged with the steering lever and managed to dodge the blasts by weaving the craft back and forth. The controls were easy enough to master. The hovercraft was steered by a handlebar that controlled the air rudders behind the fan. In smaller ships this was combined with leaning the body weight right or left. Bond was aware that good pilots used a lot of fancy footwork, but he was not familiar with it. The tricky part was keeping level. Sharp turns were almost impossible; if the ship tilted too much to one side, it would fly right into the ground. In many ways it was like flying a helicopter.

Bond took a chance and increased the speed. The two fighters pulled back between him and the mothership, and then the gunners let loose with a volley of machine-gun fire from the rear. Bullets riddled the front of

Bond's vehicle and smashed the windscreen to pieces. He ducked below the dashboard, inadvertently knocking the steering bar as he did so. His hovercraft slammed into the nearer of the two fighters, throwing the gunner off his feet. Bond regained his footing, realised what he had done, then rammed the fighter once again.

Suddenly a large concrete pyramid structure loomed ahead of his vehicle. Bond swerved just in time, coming within inches of hitting it. Looking out on the minefield, he saw that they had entered an area of the Demilitarized Zone that was otherworldly looking, surreal and frightening. The pyramid was one of many contraptions known as "tank traps"—obstructions built to prevent the progress of tanks. All around the structures were the wrecks of blown-up and burned-out tanks and other vehicles. The place looked like a postapocalyptic wasteland.

Bond forgot about his prey for the moment and concentrated on the steering as the obstacles zipped past him on either side. It was a good thing that he had logged many hours in a racing simulator at MI6. This was the kind of course one might find in a high-tech video game, where the only way around deadly obstructions was having well-honed reflexes and the ability to see the obstructions coming at a second's notice.

Bond heard more machine-gun fire coming from the hovercraft he had rammed. The gunner was back on his feet and was shooting at him again.

Why won't he stay down? Bond thought angrily as he swerved hard to slam into the fighter again. This time he forced the enemy hovercraft into one of the tank traps. The craft's skirt rode up the block, causing the fighter to tilt and slide along on its side before setting off a mine. The explosion threw the hovercraft into a fiery cartwheel. It rotated twice before rupturing into a hundred pieces.

Colonel Moon was furious. He had lost two hovercraft and the British assassin was gaining. He yelled to the pilot of the remaining fighter escort and ordered him to intercept Bond. The pilot swallowed, acknowledged the order, and turned the hovercraft around to head towards Bond, face-to-face.

Bond saw the fighter turn. He gripped the wheel and thought, *If it's a game of chicken they want . . .*

Then he felt movement behind him. The gunner he had knocked out earlier had come to and was rushing at him. Bond let go of the steering bar momentarily, turned, and slugged the gunner hard in the face. The man flew backwards, hit his head on the side of a bench, and was out cold once again.

Bond spun back to face the oncoming hovercraft. Bullets sprayed across the front of his vehicle, forcing him to duck for cover. Nevertheless, he was careful to keep the bar steady, daring the other pilot to stay on course. At the last moment the other pilot lost his nerve and swung the fighter out of the way. Bond rose from cover and guided the craft towards the mothership.

One advantage that the smaller fighter had over the mothership was speed. Bond was flying alongside the carrier in a matter of moments. The problem was that it was much larger. How was he going to stop it?

Before he had an answer, the mothership's pilot swerved and rammed Bond's hovercraft hard, pushing it towards a line of trees. Bond pulled his craft up and over, barely avoiding a collision, and found himself running parallel with the mothership on the other side of the trees. As the craft skated over a water splash, he noticed that the other fighter had turned around and was now hot on his tail.

Moon used the Tank Buster to shoot at Bond through the trees, but he only managed to shred them. He needed something more effective. He looked around at the pile of weapons at his feet, grabbed a flamethrower, and aimed it at Bond. A huge jet of fire shot out and across the trees, igniting them.

Bond was forced to drop back and steer his craft through a narrow gap in the trees, skirting around the flames. Now he was behind Moon again.

Moon shouted to his pilot to go faster, but the man didn't respond quickly enough. In frustration, Moon delivered a karate chop to the pilot's neck, pulled him out of the seat, and took over. He accelerated, then had another idea. Moon flipped a couple of switches and looked back to see if his ploy had worked.

A thick billow of black smoke poured from the back of the mothership and covered the area. Moon laughed and sped ahead.

The smoke screen effectively prevented Bond from seeing where the mothership had gone. Flying blind, he pushed straight ahead. Eventually, his craft burst out of the cloud and crashed down a fifteen-foot drop, followed by the fighter.

There were two men in the pursuing craft, which gave them an advantage in firepower. Bond used Moon's tactics by turning and shooting at the mines on the ground. These bounding fragmentation land mines were different—they were designed to leap thirty feet into the air before exploding. Bond hit one and managed to take out the gunner. Somehow the pilot kept going and pursued Bond up a narrow track, embanked on both sides.

Now the mothership appeared from nowhere and was behind both vehicles, herding them towards a massive pair of gates. They appeared to belong to the ruins of an ancient temple that stood at the end of the track.

Moon smiled as his monstrous machine bore down on Bond and the other craft.

Bond could see what was going to happen and tried to get off the track by pulling the craft sideways. But it was no good—the bank was too steep. He had only a few seconds before he was rammed into the gates.

Cursing to himself, he abandoned the controls and ran back to the rear of the hovercraft. The pursuing fighter was just a few feet behind him. Bond could see the pilot's face register confusion. Was the British spy crazy?

Either crazy or suicidal, Bond thought as he leapt from his own craft to the front of the fighter. He slammed down hard and got a grip on the windscreen. Before the pilot could react, Bond climbed over, kicked the pilot in the face, and continued to run to the rear. Now he was facing the front of the mothership. Once again, he made a death-defying leap to the nose of the larger hovercraft.

Bond's original craft crashed into the giant gates, quickly followed by the other fighter. The ensuing explosions knocked out the gates and disintegrated the two hovercraft, allowing the mothership to sail through the inferno unharmed.

The huge carrier had hurtled into the ancient temple and had nowhere to go but into the far wall. Bond threw himself over the windscreen and onto the deck as the craft smashed through, spun around on the rocks, and came to a stop.

The pilot was still unconscious. Moon had been knocked back and was stunned. Bond was surprised to find himself in one piece. He looked over at the colonel, and their eyes met. Then the hovercraft tilted sickeningly.

They had broken through the temple wall and were on the edge of a raging waterfall at least two hundred feet tall. The hovercraft had somehow lodged against some rocks.

Moon jumped up and attacked Bond. Bond rolled and threw the colonel into the side of the deck. By the time Bond was on his feet, Moon had rebounded. The two men faced each other and engaged in hand-to-hand combat. Moon was obviously experienced in martial arts, but Bond was unsure how proficient the man was. A stunning blow to Bond's chest told him everything he needed to know.

Bond fell backwards and used his feet to block Moon's kicks. He used a large case for leverage and jackknifed up and over. His right foot swung into Moon's jaw with a sickening *smack* just as the hovercraft broke free, slid further towards the edge of the cliff, and wedged between two large boulders. The jolt caused Moon to fall back against the massive fan at the back of the craft. He instinctively reached for an AK-47 at his feet.

Bond pulled a bulletproof vest from a pile on the deck and held it in front of him as he moved to the control cockpit. Moon's bullets strafed the area, hammering the vest until Bond could no longer hold it. But by then he was where he wanted to be. Bond pulled the throttles to full, causing the fan to spin. Colonel Moon was sucked off his feet and pulled against the caged propeller like a magnet. He tried to raise his gun arm away from the fan, but the suction was too strong.

The thrust was successful in dislodging the hovercraft from between the boulders. It slipped a few inches with a terrible scraping sound. In a matter of seconds, it would wrench free completely and plummet down the waterfall.

Bond looked at Moon and said, "You've met your biggest fan, Colonel." Then he ran up the craft's nose and jumped for the bank just as the suction pulled the mothership. The huge carrier toppled over and down into the white water, with Moon still attached to the fan. Bond watched as the hovercraft disappeared into the roaring void.

Gasping for breath, he closed his eyes. Bond allowed himself a brief moment to reflect on his good luck. Then he pulled himself up the bank to level ground. Out of breath and thoroughly exhausted, he stumbled back into the temple and collapsed. He lay on his back, shut his eyes again, and let himself drift.

The sounds of footsteps and guns cocking jarred him from his reverie. Bond opened his eyes to see many booted feet. He sat up and saw that dozens of soldiers had surrounded him, their guns pointed at his head. A man in a general's uniform pushed through the crowd and stood before him. He was probably in his fifties and looked very familiar. He looked grimly down at his captive.

The general addressed the soldiers but kept his eyes

23

on Bond. "My son is dead and yet the spy lives."

Bond realized who he was. General Moon. The colonel's father.

"Take him away!" the general ordered.

3

Ordeal

Pain is a great equaliser, the measure by which men and women come to grips with their inner strength. It can be both good and bad. Pain is designed as a warning that the body is being abused in some way. Pain from disease or injury can be sobering; something that one becomes either used to or not. It can be long-lasting, a harbinger of the inevitable ending of life. Occasionally, something good comes out of pain—a newborn child, but protection from the agony that can be inflicted on the human body must be counted as one of the greatest advances in medical knowledge.

Torture is man's cruellest invention. Pain inflicted upon the body by other human beings in a methodical, deliberate fashion can do just as much damage to the mind as it can to the flesh. Why else would the grand interrogators of the Spanish Inquisition torture their subjects to gain confessions? It didn't matter if those admissions were false. Brainwashing, too, is a form of torture. It can cause dedicated men to switch allegiances, give up their country's secrets, and betray their own people. The tortured will do or say anything to relieve the onslaught of hell that is systematically delivered by the tormentors. The torturing of prisoners is banned in all civilised countries because it is inhumane and barbaric. However, it is still implemented in many places around the world because it works.

James Bond was trained to withstand torture. He had undergone many instances of fiendish punishments throughout his career. It was even noted in his service record that he had the highest tolerance for pain of any Double-O agent in MI6. Nevertheless, everyone has a breaking point. His interrogators believed this. As long as they kept at it, and as long as the subject didn't die, then anything was possible. They could immerse the prisoner in freezing water several times a day for weeks. They could subject his body to the stings of black scorpions as long as there were enough to place on his skin. They could beat him as long as the men with clubs never tired. They could starve him. They could annihilate any semblance of hope for salvation.

Yet James Bond was a man who had the uncanny ability to escape within himself. By concentrating solely on the beating of his heart, Bond was capable of withdrawing from his environment into a Zen-like serenity. He could harden himself on the outside, clench his fists, and struggle against the pain, while on the inside he remained calm. If the end was near, then so be it. He had known the risks. Let them unleash their worst.

But these were not the men who would break him.

Time passed. He wasn't sure how long. Weeks turned into months, but life within the North Korean military prison seemed to be one continuous day. Or night, depending on how one looked at it. "We have all the time in the world"—well, those words certainly applied now. Bond knew that he was thinner and that his beard had grown. He felt weakened and very much alone. The cold, dingy cell where he slept was his only refuge from the suffering that existed outside the steel door.

Bond rarely thought about the past and, unlike most people, did not normally treasure memories. Those jewels of the human mind had always been anathema to his soul. But in the dark and damp cell where he had nothing but time, Bond embraced what recollections he still possessed. The exercise kept him sane—going back over his life, recounting various significant events and reimagining the sight and sound and smell of various individuals whose paths had crossed his. It was almost like outlining an autobiography in his head. He remembered the early years when his parents were alive and how his father had taught him a love for mountain climbing. His early childhood was a distant memory of love, warmth, and security. When he was eleven, his parents had died in a climbing accident. He never knew what had really happened. He was sent to live with his aunt, a charming elderly woman who doted on him and tried to give the boy the love he now so sadly lacked.

Bond recalled his teenage years at school and how he had chosen isolation over friendships. His aunt had worried that he was becoming antisocial, and she was probably right. He had not cared. Bond had immersed himself in physical discipline. He did enough schoolwork to get by so that he could have time to himself.

He finally found his calling in the Royal Navy.

He had great fondness for Sir Miles Messervy, the former M, the man who had recruited him into the Secret Service. They hadn't always agreed, but most of the time their relationship was warm and filled with mutual respect. There were others in London who meant a great deal to him—the loyal and lovely Moneypenny, good old Q, Tanner, the new M . . .

The strongest recollections from his life were centred on his work as a Double-O agent in Her Majesty's government. That first assignment, the one in which he had to assassinate an enemy operative in New York City, was his introduction to a life of great adventure and serious danger. Since then he had killed other human beings in the line of duty. He had trained himself to slough it off, bury the guilt, and pretend it didn't exist. He had hardened himself to the facts of life and death, taking each day as it came with a devil-may-care attitude. This code had kept him alive all these years.

Many faces floated through his fevered hallucinations—some of them friendly, such as Felix Leiter, Darko Kerim Bey, his friend Tiger Tanaka . . . others not so friendly, such as Ernst Stavro Blofeld, Auric Goldfinger, Dr. Julius No, Hugo Drax . . . It was important to remember them so that he could draw the line between what was good and what was evil. And then there were the beautiful and passionate women who had shared his bed—Domino, Solitaire, Tatiana, Tiffany, Honey, Kissy . . . and Tracy. They had all left their mark.

Bond's senses recalled the tastes and smells of various locations around the world, places that had left an indelible stamp on him. There was Jamaica, the island he loved more than any other; the exotic and mysterious Japan; France and its very special hideaway resort, Royale-les-Eaux; and areas in upstate New York that were stunningly beautiful in the autumn when the leaves changed colour.

The memories somehow kept him lucid and they kept him strong. He hadn't talked. He hadn't given his interrogators the satisfaction of winning. He still knew who he was, why he was there, and what he stood for.

That was all that mattered for now.

Bond had grown accustomed to the sound of boots outside the cell door. The noise automatically set his mind to work preparing his body for the day's ordeal. First came the steps, then the rattle of keys, and finally the screech of the door opening. The light from outside the cell was always blinding, nearly as painful as what Bond knew he was about to endure.

It was how he measured the passing of the days.

On this day Bond was sitting in the corner of the cell, knees folded to his chest. He was barefoot, dirty, hungry, and dazed. He looked up to see the same two guards who had come for him every other day. Two more stood behind them in the corridor.

"Something different today," one of them said in Korean.

Bond didn't move. The guard who spoke nodded to the other one. They walked over to Bond and pulled him up. One man held him from behind while the other bound his wrists. Bond didn't resist. He was beyond that now.

Once he was secure, the guards escorted him out of the cell and down the familiar hallway to the room where a little bit of him died, day after day. How much more could he take? How long would they continue to do this? What could he possibly know at this point that would be of any use to them? He wasn't sure that they wanted him to talk at all. They probably just enjoyed watching him suffer.

The guards shoved him into the torture chamber, a cold and spartan room that smelled of blood. The door slammed behind him and Bond was alone. He glanced over at the bathtub in the shadows and was surprised to find it empty. Odd. He looked to the table and saw the cageful of scorpions, but it had been set back against the wall, apparently forgotten. What was going on?

The door opened again and General Moon entered. A guard came in behind him and shut the door. Bond had not seen the general since the day he had been captured. Studying him now, Bond could see the grief for his lost son etched in his face. Somewhere behind those eyes, Bond thought he saw a trace of humanity, an inkling of compassion. Finally Moon spoke in English.

"I don't condone what they do here."

Faint memories of past defiance swam into Bond's mind. "It's not exactly five-star."

"Still you jest." Moon sighed. "Defiant to the last."

Bond said nothing.

"Your people have abandoned you," the general continued. "Your very existence denied. Why stay silent? It doesn't matter anymore. Things are out of my hands now."

Bond, with tremendous effort, managed to muster a look of resilience and slight contempt. The general waited for him to say something, anything. At last he turned to the guard and nodded. The guard opened the door and gestured for Bond to go through.

What? Bond thought. *No scorpions today? No beatings?*

They led him outside, the first real daylight he had seen in what must have been months. The brightness seared his retinas, making him squint painfully. The guard jabbed him with the barrel of an AK-47, ushering him into a waiting military transport truck.

They rode for an hour. He was alone with the general and the guard in the back of the truck. Old habits die hard, so Bond weighed his options but was forced to conclude that they had run out. He did not know why the general would bother to go to this effort before executing him and realized that he no longer cared. He allowed himself a brief, sad smile of self-congratulation. He had not been broken. Death would be his reward—and his release.

The truck stopped beside an iron bridge on the outskirts of an abandoned village. The North Korean flag flew on a large pole erected on the near side of a deep gully at the edge of which stood the burnt-out shell of a Russian T55 tank. A thick mist had settled over the land and obscured most landmarks, but Bond could make out silhouettes of tall gun towers, barbed wire, and tanks in the distance.

They made him get out and stand beside the bridge. Bond looked into the gully below and saw that it was scarred with land mines and the remains of military vehicles. The Demilitarized Zone. The fog completely screened what was beyond the bridge on the other side of the gully.

He stood complacently as six armed soldiers marched

out of the mist and lined up ten feet away from him.

So that was his retirement present. A firing squad.

The general stepped out of the truck and regarded Bond grimly. "We reach the end, Mr. Bond. Of my patience . . . and your life."

"Spare me the unpleasantries," Bond said, eyeing the six soldiers.

"I had moved us so close to peace, to unification— fifty years after the superpowers carved Korea in two," Moon said. "Then you arrive. A British spy, an assassin. Now the hard-liners have their proof that we cannot trust the West." He took a breath and continued, "You . . . took my son."

"Your firing squad should have done the job for me," Bond replied. "He was working against you, General."

"I hoped that a Western education would help him become a *bridge* between our worlds. But all it did was corrupt him."

Bond shook his head and said, "Let's get this over with."

"My son had a great ally in the West, a spy like yourself. You know it. Now, for the last time, who was it? Who made him betray his country and his name?"

"The same person who betrayed me."

Moon paused to see if Bond would reveal more. Then he said, "You choose the hard way."

"What's hard about dying, General?"

"Start walking, Mr. Bond." Moon gestured to the mist-shrouded bridge.

He had no choice. Bond set his jaw and walked res- olutely into the fog. Behind him he heard the guns cock. *At last,* he thought, *my time has come . . .*

He kept walking, waiting for the crack of gunfire,

waiting to fall in a hail of bullets. But there was nothing.

Halfway across the bridge, a figure loomed out of the mist. Another man was walking towards him. *His* hands were tied as well. The two figures grew closer until finally Bond was able to see the other man's face. It was Zao, the henchman.

A voice on a loudspeaker ordered, "Keep walking. Please keep walking."

Bond glanced back at the firing squad but saw that they were boarding the truck. Now he understood. It had been a trick to try to get him to talk. This was an *exchange*.

He returned his gaze to Zao, whose face still bore the scars made by the diamond shrapnel. From his otherwise healthy appearance, it was obvious which of the two men had been doing the harder time. They passed each other, eyes locked.

"So we're being traded," Bond said.

"It seems we are equal—in the eyes of spies," Zao acknowledged.

"Equal but not even. Your time will come."

The loudspeaker blasted again. "Keep moving!"

Zao said confidently, "Not as soon as yours . . ." He moved on, shaking his head. Bond turned slightly and watched him disappear into the fog, and then he kept walking to the other side of the gully.

Charles Robinson, MI6 special assistant to M, stood at the open border post, peering through binoculars at the bridge that spanned the Demilitarized Zone. Several military and medical personnel, including some dark-suited National Security Agency men, flanked him.

"See him?" asked the man in charge of the NSA group. His sardonic New Jersey attitude was a perfect expression of his contempt.

"Not yet, Mr. Falco," Robinson said, still scanning the bridge.

Falco was a no-nonsense security advisor to the South Koreans and had had no problem speaking his mind regarding the prisoner exchange that had been brokered between Britain and North Korea. Robinson had had just about enough of him *and* his men. He wondered why the NSA was involved at all. It was an organisation that dealt mostly with cryptology, information security, and analysing foreign signals.

"There." Robinson focused the lenses and saw Bond emerge from the swirling mist. His first thought was that the man looked like Robinson Crusoe. Double-O Seven had long hair, a beard, was covered in bruises and blisters, and was wearing rags.

Falco lifted his own binoculars to get a look and disdainfully commented, "Look at him. You'd think he was some kind of hero."

Robinson ignored the American and walked towards the bridge. Bond saw him, recognised him, and smiled through the beard. But before the two could meet, four figures in silver protective suits appeared and swarmed over Bond. One of them pressed a syringe into his arm.

Bond gladly fell into unconsciousness.

4

Impatient Patient

Bond lay unconscious and naked in the Da Vinci Machine, an ingenious device that allowed medics to scan for internal injuries, measure blood chemistry, and perform other diagnostic tests without invasive procedures. It was located in a mobile robotic operating theatre that the British armed forces could deliver to any base in the world. The one in South Korea was just outside of Seoul.

As the blue light travelled along the length of Bond's body and the table to which he was strapped slowly revolved, medics followed the results on computer screens from an observation booth.

"Widespread tissue scarring consistent with localised burns on feet and hands."

"Partial frostbite to fingers and toes."

"Extensive bruising."

"Looks like he sustained a serious injury to his left shoulder. A dislocation?"

"Yes, that occurred three years prior to his imprisonment. It's in his chart."

At one point during the examination, robotic fingers opened one of Bond's eyes and measured the dilation of his pupil with a pencil-sized beam of light. Artificial hands withdrew blood from his arm with a hypodermic.

"Strong neurotoxic traces. Probably from a venom antiserum—either Parubuthus or Death Stalker scorpion."

"My God. If it wasn't Bond, this would be an autopsy."

Test tubes spun in little machines located around the table. Thermal images of Bond's internal organs were projected onto the medics' screens.

"Blood pressure is excellent."

"Internal organs in extremely good shape, considering."

"Liver not so great."

"Well, it's definitely him, then!"

Bond didn't hear the laughter. He was dead to the world and would be for a couple more days.

Still, his heart pumped strong and steadily.

White ceiling.

Low light.

The blurry image slowly focused. His eyes darted around and saw that he was lying in a hospital bed. The room was bare, with walls of stainless steel. A single chair was fixed to the floor next to a door on the opposite wall. A man in a white coat sat there, watching him. Bond did not recognise him.

When the doctor noticed that Bond's eyes were open, he pressed a button on the wall.

Bond sat up. The grogginess went away with surprising swiftness. He felt refreshed. What had they done for him? His hands explored his body and felt no bandages or casts. He touched his face and felt the beard, but it was clean now and not matted with grime and blood.

He kicked off the sheet, swung his feet out of the bed, and sat for a moment, waiting to see if he'd lost his balance. The room didn't spin. He was fine.

The door beside the doctor opened and M stepped in. To Bond's eyes, she looked wonderful. Her bright eyes examined him and he smiled. He got to his feet and started to walk towards her when he suddenly saw a reflection of himself between the bed and where she was standing.

The room was divided by a seamless wall of reinforced, bulletproof glass.

The smile dropped from his face.

M continued to look him up and down, pausing slightly beneath his waist. Bond had forgotten that he was naked. He looked around and found a towel draped over the rail at the end of the bed. He took it and wrapped it around his lower half.

"Welcome back," M said. Her voice was filtered, relayed over a speaker.

"Such hospitality," Bond replied with some irony. He tapped the glass wall and asked, "Watching for biological agents—or double agents?"

"I take it they didn't let you have a razor?"

He fingered his stubble with distaste. "Remind me to take it up with Geneva."

The tension was palpable. It was a strange, strained situation.

"How long . . . how long was I in there?" he asked.

"Fourteen months, two weeks, and three days."

Bond felt his heart sink. *How could that be? Was it really that long?*

"I lost track after the fourteen months," he said wryly. M continued to study him, betraying no emotion. "You don't seem too pleased to see me," Bond said.

"If I'd had my way you'd still be in North Korea," she said bluntly. "Your freedom came at too high a price."

"Zao?"

She nodded. "He tried to blow up a summit between South Korea and China. Took out three Chinese agents before he was caught. And now . . . he's free."

"I didn't ask to be traded. I'd rather die in prison than let him loose."

"You had your cyanide pill," she said pointedly.

"Threw it away years ago. What the hell is this about?"

"The top American agent in the North Korean High Command was discovered and executed a week ago."

She waited for a reaction, but he refused to give her one.

"And?"

"The Americans intercepted a signal from your prison naming him."

This news hit Bond like a blow to the chest.

"And they think it was me."

There was a moment's silence before she answered.

"You were the only inmate."

He stared at her as she related the bitter facts. "They

concluded you cracked under torture and were haemorrhaging information. We had to get you out."

Now he was angry. "What do *you* think?"

M studied him for a few seconds and then turned to the doctor and said something that Bond couldn't hear. The man shook his head, but M apparently insisted. The doctor moved to the wall and pressed more buttons. A portion of the glass wall opened and M stepped through the air lock to his side.

"James," she said. "With the drugs they were giving you, you wouldn't know what you did or didn't say."

"To hell with that! I know the rules. And number one is—no deals. Get caught, you're given up. Well, I played my part. *Not* talking was all that kept me alive." He paused, his mind racing. "The mission was compromised, ma'am. Moon got a call exposing me. He had a partner in the West. Even his father knew it."

M considered this and replied, "Whether that's true or not, it's irrelevant."

"No, it isn't. The same person who set me up then has done it again—to get Zao out. So I'm going after him."

"No, Double-O Seven. You're going to our secure unit in the Falklands for evaluation."

She started for the opening in the wall and Bond said, "I exchange one cell for another—just so you can save face with the Americans?"

M stopped and turned. She eyed him evenly. "This isn't about me, Bond. Lives are at risk, and I will do *anything* to protect the integrity of the Service." She paused, took a breath, and said, "You're no use to anyone now."

As she left the room, Bond stood beside the bed. His

face settled into a picture of grim resolve.

We'll see about that, he thought.

The mobile military hospital was quiet and still at two o'clock in the morning. Most of the staff had gone to the barracks, M had left with Robinson on the long trip back to Great Britain, and the few patients staying there were asleep.

James Bond had fretted much of the day away after his humiliating meeting with his chief. He could scarcely believe that M really meant what she had said. He refused to accept that it was all over.

But for the moment there was nothing he could do. Still weak from the ordeal in North Korea, Bond went to bed and focused his mind on his heartbeat, practising the exercise he had learned to help him relax, push away stress, and slow down his metabolism. He felt his heart slow down and become tranquil. He drifted away from the hospital room, floating on his thoughts and memories again.

The medic on duty outside the observation room glanced at Bond's vital signs on the monitor. He noted that the heart rate had indeed slowed as the patient fell into a deep sleep. The young man went back to his paperback thriller and had read a few more lines when the alarm rang. Jolted by the noise, he looked at the monitor again and was stunned to see that the electronic line representing Bond's heart was moving straight and level, with no pulsating blips. He slammed his hand on the intercom button and summoned the doctor on call.

Not more than fifty seconds later, the doctor, medic, and a nurse ran into Bond's room and found him lying lifeless on the bed, his arms dangling. The doctor looked at the nurse, who understood what to do without receiving an order. She ran out and returned twenty seconds later pushing the CPR trolley. Meanwhile the doctor felt Bond's pulse and shook his head. The nurse bent over the patient and gave him the kiss of life, then alternated with the medic, who began pumping Bond's chest. For two full minutes they worked, but the EKG showed no change. The doctor finally ripped open Bond's shirt and slapped conductor gel over his chest. The medic powered up the CPR trolley and took hold of the pads.

"Are you ready?" the doctor asked. The medic nodded. "Clear!"

The medic positioned the pads just over Bond's skin and was about to make contact when the patient's eyes flicked open. Before the staff knew what was happening, they heard the heartbeat race back up to speed. In the microsecond of the medic's confusion, Bond grabbed the pads from his hands and turned them on the medic and the doctor.

The ensuing charge threw the two men across the room.

Bond swung off the bed and advanced to the open air lock. He stopped momentarily to pick up a sealed bundle of his prison clothes from a bin and looked at the astonished nurse.

"I'm checking out," he said.

He smiled disarmingly as he closed the air lock on her and the two recovering men.

"Thanks for the kiss of life," he said through the intercom.

Bond was out and away from the hospital before anyone else knew what he had done.

5

Seoul Feud

James Bond had spent little time in Seoul but knew enough about the place to blend in when and where he needed to. The semiseedy neighbourhood called Itaewon in Yongsan-gu, north of the Han River and south of Namsan Park, was famous for its bars and nightlife. A nearby military base contributed to the notoriety of this older part of central Seoul, with its a long history of cheap hotels, prostitution, and "bargain" shopping, which really meant that most of the goods were stolen. Even though there were luxury hotels and department stores in the area, Bond knew that Itaewon was the place to go for a more "colourful" consumer experience.

Bond walked through an infamous alleyway known by the locals as "hooker hill," where in the space of three minutes he was propositioned by four different women, offered leather jackets and custom-made suits by two dubious salesmen, and presented with "real" Rolex wristwatches by a teenager. He did his best to ignore the hawkers and concentrated on finding a suitable bar frequented by GIs. The smell of hot food from the stalls reminded him that he was ferociously hungry; all he had eaten in months was rubbish—and that included what he'd been served in the hospital. Unfortunately, he had very little money, and getting some was his first priority.

The Top Hat was located off the main drag in a darkened alley that probably wasn't a particularly safe place to be if one was not accustomed to the ways of the street. Luckily Bond's shabby appearance went a long way towards deflecting any interest that the common thugs might have in him.

Bond went inside the smoky bar and found that the decor did nothing to justify its incongruous name. He had once met an MI6 operative in the Top Hat many years ago and remembered that the place was busy even in the middle of the afternoon. As he had hoped, there were a dozen South Korean and four American GIs slumped over drinks or flirting with the "hostesses."

Bond sat at the bar and placed the three U.S. dollars on the counter. It was all that he had. The bartender looked at him and asked what he wanted. Bond ordered a beer, which was all he could afford. It was the first alcohol he had had since before his holiday in North Korea, and it tasted wonderful.

The GIs were noisy, harassing two young hostesses with crude comments and laughter. The girls seemed to encourage it, though, and at one point one of the Americans got up and approached a broad-shouldered man who sat beside a door leading to a rickety stairway.

Bond watched carefully as the soldier gave the man a wad of Korean won and then crooked his finger at one of the hostesses. She smiled and went with him through the door and up the stairs. The man by the door stuffed the money in his trouser pocket and continued to read the Korean newspaper he had on his lap. It was a Korean edition of *Tomorrow,* a paper that Bond assumed was under new management since its demise a few years ago.

Bond finished the beer and walked over to the man.

"How much?" he asked in English, slurring his words and pretending to be drunk.

"Go away," the man said.

"Come on, how much? I'm as good as any of these blokes."

"Get lost, or I'll smash your face in," the man said menacingly.

"What's the matter? How come I can't go upstairs, too?"

The man got off his stool and grabbed Bond by the collar. "Look, mister, get out of here. Now!" They scuffled.

"Hey, what'cha doing?" Bond protested drunkenly, putting up a pitiful defence. He purposely lost his balance and fell forward into the man, knocking them both to the floor. The pimp lost his temper and swore violently. Bond rolled on top of the man and said, "I'm so sorry, sir, forgive me, I guess I must have—"

The man kneed Bond hard in the stomach and got up, then he dragged Bond across the floor. The GIs, bartender, and the other girl watched with amusement as the pimp threw Bond outside.

"Don't come back!" the man yelled.

Bond picked himself up and staggered away, maintaining the illusion that he was hopelessly intoxicated. Once he was around the corner and out of sight, he regained his composure and pulled the clump of won that he had lifted from the pimp out of his pocket.

He counted the money and found that he had enough to buy some decent clothes, have a good meal, and perhaps bribe his way off the Korean peninsula.

M walked into the office at MI6 headquarters in London, ready to begin the day but slightly weary from the time she had spent in Korea. It had been not only a physical drain but an emotional one as well. The memory of her final conversation with Bond was unpleasant. She wasn't too sure whether to believe his story, but she also knew that she couldn't compromise her country's policies. Nevertheless, telling the man who had once been her best agent that he was no longer of any use had saddened her deeply.

As she entered her outer office, she saw that Moneypenny and Robinson were engaged in an intense conversation.

"Good morning," M announced.

They looked up, surprised, and returned the greeting.

"Welcome back, ma'am," Moneypenny said.

"You two look as if you were caught with your hands in the till. What's going on?"

Robinson and Moneypenny exchanged glances and then he spoke. "It's Double-O Seven, ma'am. He's gone."

"What do you mean, gone?"

"Escaped from the hospital. He apparently assaulted

a doctor and an orderly and left the premises. The MPs lost him on the road to Seoul."

M wasn't terribly surprised. "I wondered how long it would take. Were the doctor and orderly hurt badly?"

"Just shaken."

"Not stirred," Moneypenny added.

M glared at her and proceeded towards the door to her office. "Robinson, stay on it. I'd like to be kept informed. In the meantime, alert all of our station heads that we're looking for him."

"Yes, ma'am."

M went into the inner office and shut the door. She sighed heavily as she saw the pile of letters and reports that required her attention.

She did, however, allow herself a smile at Robinson's news.

Bond was dressed in the inexpensive dark blue knit shirt and khaki trousers that he had bought from a street vendor. Now, instead of looking like one of the homeless, he resembled a rather hip university professor who simply needed a haircut and a shave. He immediately went to an outdoor café and ordered a bowl of kimchi, a staple of the Korean diet. The dish consisted of chopped vegetables mixed with chilis, garlic, and ginger, and it was fermented in an earthenware pot. He followed this with a plate of *pulgok*—barbecued beef marinated in soy sauce, sesame oil, garlic, and chilis. To wash it down, Bond stuck with beer and tried one of the Korean brands, OB. Finally, because it had been ages since he had tasted any, he ordered *aisukurim*—ice cream—for dessert.

Feeling 110 percent better, Bond went back to the

alley where the Top Hat was located and stood in an alcove. Another bar across the street looked promising, but first Bond took stock of his funds. He had the equivalent of a hundred and forty pounds in Korean won. It would have to do.

He watched several servicemen go into the GI Joe, the establishment across the road. Like the Top Hat, it was rowdy and smoky, inhabited mostly by South Koreans in naval uniforms. Bond took a seat near them and ordered another beer. They spoke fast but were loud enough for him to catch much of what they were saying. One sailor with a rose tattoo on his forearm was complaining about having to go to Hong Kong again in the morning and that he would miss his girlfriend. The others taunted him with obscene jokes. The sailor insulted them in return and they laughed in good fun.

After a while, a rough-looking civilian entered the bar and looked over the clientele. He saw the tattooed man, went to him, and asked about some money.

"I don't have it, I'll pay you when I get back from Hong Kong," Mr. Tattoo said.

"I bet you just spent a hundred dollars U.S. on drinks!" the other man complained. "I think you had better cough up the money tonight. You may not come back from Hong Kong!"

"I'll be back, don't worry; my girlfriend is here."

The civilian cursed the man's girlfriend and pulled a gun. He held it to the sailor's head and said, "You're not going to make it *to* Hong Kong unless you pay me my money."

The bartender shouted, "Take your feud outside or I will call the police!" The other sailors stood, ready for a fight. The man with the gun threatened to shoot the tattooed man if his friends came closer.

"It's all right," Mr. Tattoo said to the other sailors as he stood. "This man is a friend of mine. We have to settle a business deal."

"Let's go outside," the civilian said. He shoved the tattooed man outside and turned to the others. "Leave us alone."

As soon as they were outside, Bond got up and nonchalantly went after them. He stepped into the dark alleyway, looked around, but didn't see anyone. Then he heard some hushed arguing not far away. Bond quietly walked towards the two men until he could see the civilian's back. The gun was in the sailor's face, and the man was clearly terrified.

Bond tapped the gunman on the shoulder and said, "Excuse me."

The thug turned around and caught a staggering blow in the nose. Bond quickly disarmed the man, kneed him in the stomach, and rammed his head into the wall. The creep fell to the ground, unconscious.

The sailor looked at Bond with awe and suspicion.

"I couldn't help overhearing. If you need some money, I have a proposition for you," Bond said.

The sailor shook his head. "Get out of here," he said. "Don't you know who that was?"

"No, and I really don't care."

"That was Kim Dong, a very dangerous man!"

Bond regarded the hoodlum on the ground, said, "He doesn't look like much of a threat to me," and turned back to the bar. The sailor warily followed him inside and they sat at the counter. His friends started to get up and come over to him, but the sailor waved them away.

Bond slapped the rest of his won on the counter.

"This is twice what you owe and it's all I have. But if you can get me on your ship tonight and take me to Hong Kong, it's yours," Bond said.

"Are you crazy? How am I going to do that?"

"You have a duffel bag, don't you? Part of your gear?"

"Yes . . ." The man looked dubious.

"I'll hide inside. You carry me aboard and let me get out of the bag where I can't be seen. I promise you I'll get out of your way and you won't see me again for the entire trip. I used to be in the Royal Navy—I know ships. I can find a safe hiding place and no one will find me. And if they do, you won't be implicated."

"I don't know . . ."

"All right, I'll double it after I get to Hong Kong," Bond said. "Just give me your name and outfit details and I'll wire the money to you."

"What, you give your word, as a 'gentleman'?" the man asked sceptically.

"Absolutely."

"You're mad. Why should I trust you?"

"Why did I stick out my neck for you just now?"

"Because you're crazy!"

Bond smiled. "Maybe I am. But not like you think."

They went to the base, which was located west of Seoul near Inchon. A sizeable fleet was stationed there, and the South Koreans used it to make frequent patrols around the peninsula, to Japan, and around the Chinese mainland to Hong Kong. The sailor, whose name was Chae, made Bond wait outside the compound so that he could go to the barracks and retrieve his duffel bag. An hour later, he returned and put the bag on the ground.

"I put clean clothes in it to help pad it out," Chae said.

"I appreciate it," Bond said as he climbed in. Chae stuffed the extra clothing around Bond's body and tied the end.

"Can you breathe?" Chae asked.

"I'll live," Bond's muffled voice replied.

Chae heaved the heavy bag over his shoulder and went back inside the compound, explaining to the sentry that his girlfriend had bought him a lot of new clothes.

The sailors had to be ready at five o'clock in the morning. Chae waited until the last minute to load the duffel bag into the transport vehicle so that Bond would be on top of the pile. Chae climbed in with the other sailors, and the truck left the compound for the short ride to the wharf where the *Po Hang*–class corvette was docked. Fully armed with torpedoes, a variety of guns and missiles, depth charges, and decoys, the eighty-eight-metre-long battleship was a typical vessel of the South Korean fleet.

Chae carried Bond on board, then immediately went below to make his way to his quarters. A number of other sailors crowded the passageways, so Chae reversed his route and headed for the mess, took another turn, and ended up in the laundry facility. No one was around there. He placed the bag on the floor and untied it.

"You just better not be caught," Chae said.

"I won't. Thank you, Chae," Bond said as he climbed out.

Chae gave Bond two packages of rations. "Here, you might need these. It's two days to Hong Kong."

"Much obliged," Bond said. "I'll be sure to wire you that money."

"Forget about it," Chae said. "Before we left, I heard that Kim Dong has a broken nose. That's worth it."

Chae took his bag and quickly left the room, leaving Bond standing amidst piles of sheets and towels. As a former naval officer, Bond knew exactly how to stow away on board ship. The trick was to keep moving, never staying in one place for very long, and, of course, to leave no telltale traces.

The empty torpedo tube was a perfect place to recline. It reminded Bond of a sensory deprivation chamber, albeit a rather cold and damp one. It usually held a 324-mm MK-32 torpedo, but luckily today the compartment happened to be empty. Sleep came easily to him. His body still had a long way to go to reach recovery, and deep slumber was what he needed. The sounds and smells of the battleship faded away as Bond floated into a state of rapid eye movement and his subconscious began to take over. An indication that a dream was in progress, REM is marked by inactivity—save for the eye movement. Bond rarely remembered his dreams, but he had one that night that was both disturbing and inauspicious.

He was back in the North Korean prison. Strangely, the all-too-familiar cell felt like home.

The sound of booted footsteps echoed in the hallway and the iron door creaked open. Colonel Moon stood in the doorway with an odd smile spreading across his face, as if he knew something that Bond didn't. Bond stood and said, "I'll follow you, since you're dead." He walked behind the colonel to the torture room, where

51

more things were not quite right. Instead of ice cubes in the bathtub, there were diamonds. The scorpions in the cage had become leaves. Colonel Moon had changed as well—he was now wearing a mask. Or rather, the man in the North Korean uniform was wearing a mask that resembled the *face* of Colonel Moon.

Bond suddenly found himself strapped to the torture table, in agony. He didn't know what was causing the pain. He squinted at the man with the Colonel Moon mask and demanded, "Who are you?"

The man laughed and tore off the mask to reveal a completely blank face—smooth and fleshy, with no eyes, nose, or mouth—nothing. It was one of the most horrible images Bond had ever seen.

He woke with a start, realised where he was, and breathed deeply. As the dregs of the nightmare trickled away, Bond settled back into his hiding place and went back to sleep.

6

Stopover in Hong Kong

Wet and bedraggled, James Bond climbed up a quay on the Kowloon side of Victoria Harbour and caught his breath. The mile-long swim from the South Korean military ship had been the most difficult part of his journey. The two days had passed relatively quickly and with no untoward events. As was his plan, Bond had hidden in storage rooms, but mostly he had stayed in a torpedo tube that had been surprisingly comfortable. When the ship arrived in the harbour, he simply went up on deck and dived into the warm, green water before anyone could stop him.

Now that he was ashore, it was time to get things moving. Hong Kong had always been one of Bond's favourite cities and this hadn't changed after it returned to Chinese rule in 1997. Colonial life remained if one looked hard enough for it. It was a place dedicated to the pursuit of profit and pleasure.

Bond walked from the quay to the Rubyeon Royale, one of the world's top hotels. He had stayed there often and the manager was a friend. Occupying a prime location overlooking the harbour, the hotel was in the very heart of Hong Kong's business and entertainment district. It was surrounded by well-tended gardens that had been modelled after landscapes in England and displayed a striking mixture of Chinese and British design schemes.

He went inside to the registration desk and said, "My usual suite, please."

The supercilious clerk looked him up and down and said, "I'm sorry, sir, do you have any luggage or . . . credit card?"

Before Bond could reply, a familiar voice interrupted. "Mr. Bond! So good to see you. It's been a long time."

A middle-aged Chinese man stepped out of the office and said to the clerk, "Open the Presidential Suite."

Bond shook hands with him. "Mr. Chang. Perhaps you could send up my tailor. And some food."

"The lobster's good. May I suggest quail's eggs, rice, and sliced seaweed?"

"And if there's any left—the '61 Bollinger?"

"And a barber?"

"Good idea."

Chang leaned in close and whispered conspiratorially, "Been busy, have we, Mr. Bond?"

Bond smiled and replied, "Just surviving, Mr. Chang."

•   •   •

Three hours later, Bond put down his Philishave. He examined himself in the mirror and decided that the haircut he had received earlier wasn't too bad. He looked almost like his old self. The bruises were still there, but he felt like a new man. There was a knock at the door. Wrapping a towel around his waist, Bond stepped out of the bathroom and walked past the bed, on which a fabulous array of new shirts was spread. He paused at the table in the sitting room, plucking a grape from the display that included fruit, caviar, and champagne.

Bond opened the door to find a gorgeous young Chinese girl wearing a terry-cloth robe and carrying a gym bag.

She batted her long eyelashes and said, "I am Peaceful Fountains of Desire. The masseuse. I come with compliments of the manager."

Bond took a second to take her in. "I'm sure you do."

He ushered her inside, checking her out as she put down the bag. The girl removed some oil from her bag, beckoned him into the bedroom, and indicated the bed.

"Facedown, please."

Bond moved the shirts, then stepped close to her, smiling. He put his arms around her, but she said, "I'm not that kind of masseuse." Before she could pull away, he slipped his hand beneath her robe and pulled out a concealed Beretta.

He held it against her and said, "I'm not that kind of customer."

"Please . . . It's for my own protection," she stammered.

Noticing that her eyes kept darting to the full-length

mirror that took up a large part of a wall, Bond pulled away but kept the gun trained on her. He picked up a heavy ashtray from the dresser and lobbed it at the mirror, shattering it. Mr. Chang and three heavies stood in a darkened room, surrounded by banks of recording equipment. Their shock gave way to embarrassment.

"My," Bond said. "A room with a view. You think I haven't always known you were Chinese intelligence, Mr. Chang?"

The manager stepped into the room, now sullen—far from his usual grovelling self.

"Hong Kong is our turf now, Bond."

"Don't worry, I haven't come to take it back."

With the gun, Bond directed the heavies towards the door. They looked at Chang, who nodded. After the men left the room, Chang asked, "What the hell do you want?"

"Just to help you settle a score. A terrorist named Zao killed three of your men recently. Get me into North Korea and I'll take care of him for you."

Chang made a face, unconvinced. "What's in it for you?"

"A chance to reminisce. Zao has information I need."

Chang was still unsure, but Bond surprised him by returning the Beretta. "Consider it a favour to your country. I'm . . . working freelance on this," he said.

"I, um, will have to ask Beijing," Chang said.

"Do it. Now get out." Bond looked at Peaceful and said, "You, too, unless you really want to give me a massage."

She pouted and joined an irritated Chang. Together they left the room.

56

Bond decided to reward himself with a glass of his favourite vintage champagne. He was back in business.

Later in the evening a large envelope was delivered to Bond's suite. He was pleased to find that it contained a full dossier on Zao and a note from Chang that read, "Checkout time is twelve noon tomorrow. Please be prompt." Bond took that to mean that his request would be granted.

He poured another glass of Bollinger and reclined on the couch with the dossier. He had pulled the curtains open earlier, revealing a magnificent view of the city's splendid, colourful skyline. The suite was on a floor high enough to escape the noise of the traffic, but low enough to take in the flashing neon that characterized Hong Kong at night.

Zao had an interesting background. Born Tan Ling Zao, he was the eldest of six children. His father was North Korean, but his mother was Chinese. There wasn't much in the report concerning Zao's childhood, save for the mention of an early arrest at the age of nine for setting fire to a South Korean Jeep. Since the act was viewed as somewhat patriotic, he was let off with a warning. His military service was distinguished, and he had excelled as a member of a Special Forces unit. This experience had taught him unorthodox methods of killing, and going by the evidence in the file, he was alarmingly good at it. At the age of twenty-one, he was recruited into the Reconnaissance Bureau of the General Staff Department, an organisation responsible for collecting strategic, operational, and tactical intelligence for the Ministry of the People's Armed Forces. The unit also boasted of infiltrating intelligence personnel into

South Korea through tunnels under the Demilitarized Zone and by sea. Zao spent six years working as a spy, but to all intents and purposes he was really a terrorist. At least fourteen incidents in South Korea were attributed to him, including three assassinations, six bombings, and one kidnapping. When he was twenty-eight, he was discharged from the service and went to work as a freelance agent for various military groups. It was believed that he was still secretly employed by the Reconnaissance Bureau, which farmed him out to different factions within the armed forces for his expertise in guerrilla warfare and methods of intimidation. He practised the kind of tactics that would never be condoned by the Geneva Convention, and because of this he was in high demand.

A sick character, Bond thought. His former boss, Colonel Moon, was not much better. What Chinese intelligence knew about him was sketchy, too, except for the period of time Moon spent in Great Britain. He had spent four years at Oxford before travelling to America to study at Harvard. Moon had enjoyed the reputation of having radical ideas that he hadn't been afraid of expressing. He was asked to leave Oxford for "inciting unrest." After his time at Harvard, Moon went back to North Korea and, with his father's influence, quickly became an army officer. Once he was established as a colonel with his own legion of followers, Moon broke away from the more moderate path his father had taken towards bringing about peace between the two Koreas. The younger Moon supported a more aggressive stance, and he was not above participating in criminal enterprises to fund his endeavours—trading arms for conflict diamonds, for example, so that he could then use the diamonds to buy his way into other areas of nastiness. No one really knew what Moon had been spending his wealth on, but intelligence sources feared that he was developing a nuclear or biological capability.

After a restful night and an exquisite breakfast, Bond was refreshed and ready to go. He approached the front desk and found Chang back to his normal deferential self.

"Ah, Mr. Bond. I have a little something for you. To thank you for gracing us with your presence."

He lifted an elaborate Chinese box on to the counter. Bond opened it to find a passport, money, and a freighter ticket to Havana.

"Cuba?" Bond asked.

"It seems that Mr. Zao has lost himself in Havana." Chang smiled. "And here's something else I thought you might be able to use." He placed an object wrapped in brown paper next to the box. Bond picked it up and immediately recognised the feel and weight of a Walther P99.

"There are four magazines to go with it," Chang said.

"I'm much obliged. I owe you one, Chang."

"Don't mention it. When you see Zao, say good-bye from us."

Bond gathered his presents and said, "I'll be happy to deliver the message."

7

Jinxed

Bond felt ambivalent about Cuba. The largest island in the Caribbean, once the jewel of the Spanish Empire, Cuba has great natural beauty and still preserves many architectural treasures for the colonial era. But unlike Bond's beloved Jamaica, where even crime and political unrest cannot spoil the island's vibrant way of life, Cuba, stifled by its lack of personal freedom, has a pervasive air of mistrust and suspicion. The only Communist country in the western hemisphere is isolated from both the nearby United States and its Caribbean-island neighbours: its closest ally is Russia, even though the latter has abandoned the Communist way of life that originally brought them together. It is a hotbed of intrigue and artifice—and a haven for spies and others who need to hide their activities from the world's eyes.

The trip from the Far East had been uneventful and

frustrating. The freighter ride had taken far too long. Anything could have happened in that time. Zao might have left Cuba, M could have changed her mind about 007, and hell might have frozen over. Impatient and restless, Bond planned to waste no more valuable time once he got into the country. After leaving the ship, he paid a taxi driver to take him to the centre of the big city.

Regardless of the political climate in Cuba, Havana was indeed beautiful, perhaps the most attractive city in the Caribbean. Winston Churchill once said that he "might leave his bones there," and that it was a place where "anything might happen." Indeed, it was a city full of mystery, conspiracy, and romance. The streets were full of dark-eyed sirens and men wearing Panama hats and white linen suits.

He entered the cobbled paths of Habana Vieja, the oldest part of the city, where Ernest Hemingway once had a home not unlike the Hemingway House in Key West, Florida. It was a seductive area within fortified walls, full of Spanish Colonial buildings, convents, Baroque churches, and castles that reminded Bond of Madrid. As he moved along a busy long-decayed street that ran parallel with the harbour channel, the smell of tobacco wafted from his destination—a warehouse that bore the sign RAOUL'D CIGARS. He went inside, where Cubans were hard at work processing tobacco leaves on long tables. Beautiful young women rolled cigars on their inner thighs. Very little light filtered in from the outside through slats in the windows. Bond approached the desk at the front of the factory and addressed the old man sitting behind it.

"I'm here to pick up some Delectados."

The man looked surprised. "We haven't made Delectados for thirty years."

Bond gave him a card. "Universal Exports. Check with your boss."

Shaking his head, the old man lifted an ancient telephone and made a call. He spoke in rapid Spanish as Bond looked around the room. The workers had taken a break and were participating in an afternoon karaoke session. One of the young girls was belting out a Caribbean tune, accompanied by an old battered ghetto blaster.

The old man hung up and said, "Your passport, please." Bond handed it to him, then followed him towards some stairs. They went up two flights to the roof of the building, where another man sat at a table under the shade of a canopy. He was using an eyepiece to study the bejewelled handle of an antique knife. The Havana cityscape spread out behind him in all its glory.

Raoul hadn't changed much. Bond guessed that he must be around sixty by now. He wondered if the man would recognise him. It had been a long time.

The old man handed Raoul the passport and then drew a gun from a holster on his belt. He stood off to one side and watched his boss examine the passport. Raoul beckoned for Bond to sit in the chair facing the table. After a moment he handed the passport back to Bond, considered him for a few seconds, then reached down to retrieve a box of cigars marked DELECTADOS. Using the knife, he slit the bind and said, "I'd come to think the Delectados would never be smoked."

He removed a cigar and nipped the tip. "They are particularly hazardous for one's health, Mr. Bond. Do you know why?"

Bond completed the code by replying, "It's the addition of the Volado tobacco. Slow burning. It never goes out."

"Just like a sleeper."

"Sorry for the rude awakening."

Raoul lit the cigar and took a drag. He exhaled and said, "I'm not sure if I am happy to see you again, Mr. Bond. It has been a long time."

"Indeed."

"You know, I always thought I would relish this. But now that I finally taste it, I find the flavour too strong." He took another puff and then said, "I love my country, Mr. Bond."

"I wouldn't ask you to betray your people. I'm after a North Korean."

Bond could see that this information was a great relief to Raoul, although the man remained guarded.

"A tourist?" Raoul asked.

"A terrorist."

"One man's terrorist is another man's freedom fighter."

"Zao has no interest in freedom."

Raoul stared at Bond for another moment, puffing on the cigar. He then said something in Spanish to the other man, who put away his gun.

"Will you share a drink with me?" he asked Bond.

Bond nodded and Raoul pulled two glasses out of a drawer, along with an unmarked liqueur bottle. He poured the cloudy brown liquid and handed a glass to Bond.

"I still have some friends in high places," Raoul said as he held up his glass.

"Cheers." Bond smiled as he savoured the distinctive flavour of thirty-year-old Havana rum.

Raoul unrolled an old map of Cuba and placed a lit candlestick on one end and a microscope on the other to hold it down on the table.

The sun had set and the workers had gone home. Bond and Raoul had eaten dinner together. The tamales were highly spiced. They were made with freshly ground corn with pieces of pork mixed in with the dough. These were complemented with hot Cuban bread, which was crispy on the outside and lightly textured on the inside. After several glasses of rum, the old cigar maker was in a good mood. He excused himself, went into his office for an hour to make some phone calls, and then beckoned Bond to join him in the cool; shady room that was crowded with bric-a-brac.

"Favours called in, some dollars spread about—we find your friend is in Los Organos." Raoul pointed to the spot on the map. "Perhaps he is sick. There's a clinic there, on an island."

"What kind of clinic?"

"It's run by a Dr. Alvarez. He supposedly leads the field in gene therapy. You know, increasing the life expectancy of . . . well, our beloved leaders and the richest Westerners. We may have lost our freedom in the revolution, but we have a health system second to none."

Bond glanced about the office and noted the delicate weighing scales and other antiques.

"You don't seem to have done too badly out of the revolution," he said.

"We all have our ways of getting by. You'd be surprised how many government officials come to me for little reminders of the decadent times."

"Nothing wrong with a little decadence."

Bond took a pair of binoculars from a shelf and blew the dust off them. He peered through them and found that they were in perfect condition; the lenses just needed a bit of cleaning. Next to a faded map of the nearby island San Monique lay an old book that caught Bond's eye as well. He picked it up and saw that it was *Field Guide to Birds of the West Indies* by a respected ornithologist.

"Mind if I borrow these?" he asked Raoul.

The cigar maker shrugged and nodded. "My sources tell me this Zao is very dangerous. I wish I could give you more help."

"I understand. There's just one last thing. I could do with a fast car."

Raoul thought a minute and replied, "I think I might have something."

Just before sundown, the cream-and-beige 1957 Ford Fairlane 500 hardtop retractable convertible rolled into the mountainous and lush Sierra de los Organos region in Pinar del Río, Cuba's westernmost province. Cuba has an unsurpassed collection of American cars from the 1950s—an unexpected result of her long exclusion from the American market. Even though its exhaust tended to backfire every twenty miles or so, Bond took real pleasure in driving the elderly but beautifully restored car.

Bond had left Havana on the Autopista, a six-lane national highway that bisected the island and then turned northward to skirt around the Parque Nacional

La Gúira. From there he crossed into the mountains and drove through overgrown tropical mesas, the map, binoculars, and field guide on the seat next to him, until he reached the small hotel located on the northwest coast that Raoul had "recommended."

The place was a decaying colonial remnant called Hotel de los Organos. It was surrounded on three sides by trees, and behind it was the expansive Caribbean, dotted with a few small islands in the distance. There were a couple of small craft moored to the quay just beyond the beach lounge area. The hotel looked like a modest vacation spot, but Bond knew it was the clientele registered there who made it special.

His information was confirmed when he took a look at the register that was sitting on the front desk in the empty lobby. The names were all aliases—Mr. Jones, Mr. Smith . . . When no one appeared after a few moments, he rang the bell. A clerk eventually stuck his head out of an office from which came the low sound of a radio playing a cover version of "California Girls." The clerk hurried to take Bond's money. Bond signed the register with his real name and paid in cash. The clerk turned to the wall behind him and selected a key just as a burly creep with a South African accent stormed into the lobby. He smelled, was smoking a cigar, and bumped into Bond as he approached the desk.

"My suite ready yet?" he demanded.

The clerk jumped and said, "Ah, yes, Mr. Krug. Suite 42. For one night. It will be ready in ten minutes. If you—"

Krug leaned over the counter and grabbed the clerk by his tie. "What kind of place are you running here?

Get it done. Now!" He pushed the man away and knocked Bond again as he stomped off. Ruffled now, the clerk gave Bond his room key and pointed the way. Bond thanked him and walked through the lobby, where a parrot in a cage called out, *"Dame un beso!"* A few wheelchairs were folded and stacked against the wall.

He went through a door and down a boarded walkway to the fan-swept beach lounge area, where many men were sitting in the shade and passing the time. They were well dressed and overmuscled. Some Colombians lounged around a television set. Europeans played with Game Boys. Bond recognised some Serbian wiseguys hunched around a game of speed chess. Apparently a lot of waiting happened here and not much else. The criminal air of the gathering was not lost on Bond, but neither was the boredom and apathy. Not one man bothered to look up at him when he entered. It was bizarre.

Krug, the South African creep with no manners, pushed past Bond once again to greet an acquaintance standing at the bar. After a while a waiter approached the man and said, "Mr. Krug, the papers for your appointment tomorrow at the clinic."

Krug took them from the waiter and said, "About bloody time, Fidel. Now round up some girls and send them to Room 42." He pulled a pistol and pointed it at the waiter's crotch. "Unless you wanna be Fidel Castrato, quick, quick, quick!" The waiter hurried off as Krug and his pal laughed.

Bond stepped outside to the terrace and looked at the sea. Isla Organos, the island he was interested in, was just off the coast. He peered through the binoculars and saw the ruins of an old sea fort high up on the island. Extending from the dilapidated structures was a modern medical complex. Patients were being wheeled about by orderlies dressed in white, which explained the wheelchairs in the hotel lobby. Bond focused the binoculars on a sign that read THE ALVAREZ CLINIC.

He moved the field glasses down to the quay at the foot of the island and noticed that there were a few armed guards standing around. Armed guards for a medical clinic? What was wrong with this picture?

Bond swung the binoculars to the quay behind the hotel and his eyes caught movement in the water. There was someone swimming towards shore—a girl. Bond lowered the binoculars and watched her emerge and walk up the beach towards the terrace. She was wearing an orange bikini that revealed a stunning figure. The girl was dark-skinned and lithe, with short dark hair. She picked up a towel from the sand and came up to the terrace, drying her hair. Bond pretended not to be interested and raised his binoculars again to look at the glorious sunset. She joined him, looking out at the horizon and smiling at the vista.

"Magnificent view," Bond said, lowering the field glasses.

"Yes, it is," she said. "Though it seems to be lost on everyone else."

American accent. Interesting, Bond thought. Now that she was up close, he could see that she was truly beautiful. She had large brown eyes and long, pixielike eyelashes. Her beauty had a beguiling purity and was enhanced by the glow of the evening light.

A waiter appeared at the door to the terrace and asked if they wanted anything.

Bond ordered a Mojito, a Cuban drink made from two ounces of light rum, one ounce of lime juice, two teaspoons of sugar, a small handful of spearmint, and soda water that was served in a tall glass.

"I'll have the same," the girl added. The waiter went off and she offered her hand to Bond. "Giacinta. My friends call me Jinx."

"My friends call me James Bond." They shook hands. "Jinx?"

"Born on Friday the thirteenth."

"You believe in bad luck?"

"Let's just say my relationships don't seem to last."

"I know the feeling."

They heard screeches of birds and animals coming from the dense foliage surrounding the hotel. Bond glanced back at the thugs in the bar.

"The predators all appear at sunset," he commented.

She looked him over again as the drinks arrived. When the waiter had left, she asked, "And why is that?"

Bond took a sip and replied, "It's when their prey comes out to drink."

She threw a quick look at the glass in her hand.

"Too strong for you?" Bond asked.

Was it a reference to her drink or to his approach? She looked him in the eye and said, "I could grow to like it." She paused briefly before adding, "If I had the time."

Was that a hint of regret? Bond wondered. "How much time have you got?"

"Oh, at least until dawn. What about you?"

"I'm just here for the birds." He indicated the binoculars. "Ornithologist."

"Now there's a mouthful."

They knew they were sharing the same emotions and reactions. Curiosity. Suspicion. Attraction. She looked out to the last rays of the dying sun.

"So shouldn't you be off with the owls or something?" she asked.

"No owls in Los Organos. Nothing to see till the morning. Not out there, anyway."

She felt his eyes on her in the near dark. As she looked back at him with a level gaze, she asked, "And what do the predators do after the sun's gone down?"

Their eyes locked. "They feast," Bond said, "like there's no tomorrow."

She held the gaze and her eyes suddenly glinted with approval and anticipation.

Jinx fell away from him, spent, flushed with passion. Bond's eyes glowed with the memory of their shared pleasure. The moonlight streamed through the open window of his hotel room and fell upon her glistening bronze body. She was magnificent, a perfect specimen of female beauty.

"Are you always so frisky?"

"I've been missing the touch of a good woman," Bond replied.

Smiling, she leaned out of bed and fished something out of her discarded clothes. Then, with a deft flick of her wrist, a blade flashed in the light as it snapped into position. Bond's heart leaped and he almost struck out at her until he saw that she was merely dissecting a fig held in her other hand.

"Who says I'm good?" she asked. She parted the fruit, ran her tongue through the exposed flesh, and pre-

70

sented it to Bond. He ate it out of her hand and she licked the fig seeds from her lips.

He eyed her and tossed aside the rest of the fig. "So show me your other side."

8

The Beauty Parlour

Bond was normally a light sleeper, but he slept soundly after the long and adventurous night with Jinx. When the shafts of sunlight from the window hit his face, he stirred and turned to the other side of the bed, and saw that the space was empty. He hadn't heard her leave, which was unusual for him.

He got up and looked out the window at the quay behind the hotel. One of the boats was evidently preparing to launch towards Isla Organos. Several of the heavies from the bar were aboard. Jinx came into view, handed documentation to a guard on the quay, then climbed on board with the others.

What is she up to? Bond wondered.

He dressed hurriedly, grabbed his things, and rushed down to the lobby. The line of folded wheelchairs was still there. He took one, went back up the stairs, and found Room 42. He knocked loudly three times before he heard Krug's angry voice.

"Who the hell is it?"

"Room service," Bond replied. He heard some muffled cursing and some scuffling before the door opened. Krug was wearing a bathrobe.

"What the hell do you want? I didn't order room service." He looked at the chair. "You got the wrong room! I don't need no goddamn wheelchair!"

Bond slugged him hard in the face. The burly man fell back into the room, out cold.

"You do now," Bond quipped.

He scanned the corridor to make sure that no one had seen him, and then he went into the room for a quick search. Bond found the man's jacket draped over a chair. Krug's papers were inside the pocket.

He quickly unfolded the wheelchair and heaved the man into it. Posing as an orderly, Bond wheeled the unconscious thug out of the room and down to the wharf outside. The first boat had already departed, but a second one was beginning to fill. Bond presented Krug's papers to the uninterested guard, then wheeled the South African onto the boat.

The trip took a short ten minutes. Guards on the island's wharf inspected every arrival's documentation with halfhearted interest. Once he was past security, Bond wheeled Krug up a ramp and into the building. They boarded a lift and rode it up to the clinic's main entrance. A pretty receptionist greeted Bond and took the papers. She smiled, handed them back, and said in Spanish, "Wait in the hall. Someone will come for him."

Bond returned the smile and headed down the cor-

ridor with the wheelchair. Windows lined the passageway, providing a spectacular view of the sea far below.
Bond estimated that the clinic was two hundred feet
above the sea.

He reached an intersection. Ahead of him was a small
sun-filled quad where a few patients sat quietly in
wheelchairs. To his left, steps led down to another passage and a set of double doors. The words PROHIBITED
AREA were printed on one of the doors. The second one
was open, and Bond could see a guard on the other side
of the threshold, reading a newspaper. Two medics
came out of a side door and headed through the open
door. The guard acknowledged them and then they
turned a corner at the end of the passage.

Bond wheeled Krug into the quad and looked out one
of the open windows. By scanning down and across, he
could see the side of the building where the prohibited
area was. There were some open windows along the
facade. Climbing down there wouldn't be too difficult
as long as he could cause a distraction.

Bond pushed the wheelchair back to the intersection,
shoved it roughly down the steps towards the guard,
and ran back into the quad. The wheelchair crashed to
the level below and Krug spilled out onto the floor. The
guard hurried to help him, along with a medic from the
door on the side.

The commotion got the attention of the other patients
in the quad, giving Bond an opportunity to slip out of
the open window, grasp a railing, and swing down a
level on the outside of the building. Supported by a
shallow iron ledge, he inched his way to the first open
window and climbed in. It was a private room. An elderly man hooked up to a heart monitor was asleep in

his bed. Bond quietly crossed the floor, taking a grape as he left the room.

He was now in the prohibited area beyond the double doors. The guard and medic were still fussing with Krug off to the left and didn't notice Bond moving quickly in the opposite direction. He turned the corner and was confronted by a dead end.

Where have those two medics gone?

Bond looked directly above him and noticed a security camera pointing across the passage at a wall covered by a floor-to-ceiling mural of three Cuban Communist icons—Fidel Castro, Che Guevara, and Camilo Cienfuegos. Keeping close to the wall, Bond reached up and twisted the camera lens out of focus. He then examined the artwork, ran his hand over the paint, and found that the star on Che's cap was not flush with the wall. Bond turned it clockwise and the mural split, exposing a doorway. He stepped through into a blue light.

He found himself in a chamber lined with revolving mirrored columns, like a shrine to DNA's double helixes. He followed the passage until he heard whispering from beyond an open door. Bond stepped inside the room and quietly peered through the plastic curtains surrounding a bed. An old man was asleep. Over the beeps and scratches of the medical equipment, a language tape droned in French and English. It sounded like a simple language teaching aid.

What is Zao doing in this place?

Bond went back to the passageway and continued on to the next open door. Behind the plastic curtains in this room was a female patient who seemed to be in a strange kind of half sleep. A curved screen covered her face. Lights on the contraption pulsated randomly, and again a language tape whispered in Russian then German.

Bond moved closer, bent down, and tried to see the woman's face underneath the screen. It was very close to her, but he could see that her eyes were fluttering. REM—rapid eye movement. She was dreaming in a very intense way. Could this machine be inducing dreams?

What kind of doctor was this Dr. Alvarez?

Bond moved on. He was about to go into another patient's room when he heard footsteps behind him. He quickly slipped through another open door and waited until two medics passed. Bond emerged, looked both ways, and continued exploring. Finally he heard what he was searching for—a Korean voice. Bond crossed into the dimly lit room, which was full of high-tech equipment. There was a man in the bed, hooked up to a moving-graph EKG, tubes, and other devices. Another "Dream Machine" covered his face. His voice tape was translating Korean into English.

Bond moved closer to the bed. He had to know. He carefully slid the Dream Machine back and found himself staring at an unnaturally pale man who looked strangely familiar. Bond scrutinised the face more closely and then he understood.

It was Zao, but he had been radically altered. He appeared unfinished, as if the raw material of humanity had not yet been given final shape.

So that was it. The gene therapy practised at the clinic was for remodelling people. It was the perfect way to change one's identity and disappear; the ultimate escape. No wonder so many hardened criminals were coming there from all over the world. They could get new bodies, new faces, and new languages—whatever they wanted.

Bond grabbed hold of the drips feeding into Zao and bunched them into a knot, cutting off the supply. Nothing happened for several seconds. Then, suddenly, Zao opened his eyes. The pupils were unnaturally blue and reptilian.

The terrorist jerked upright and hissed with pain.

"Good," Bond said. "I got your attention."

Zao looked at Bond in disbelief. Bond gripped the drip tubes tighter, held them in one hand, and drew his Walther. He placed the barrel next to Zao's temple.

"Who's bankrolling your makeover, Zao?" he demanded. "The same person who set me up in North Korea?"

Zao's right arm swung around. Bond felt pain on his shoulder and dropped the pistol. It slid across the room and ended up under an MRI machine. Zao held a scalpel in his hand, freshly dripping with Bond's blood. Bond reflexively knocked over a drip stand that fell on top of Zao, breaking one of the mobile lights. But the terrorist recovered and leapt off the bed. He lunged at Bond, dragging along the machines, drips, and EKG trolley. Bond picked up a steel pan and smashed him in the head. Zao blocked a second blow with the plastic curtain.

Bond went for Zao's scalpel hand and caught it, and then the two men somersaulted over the bed. Zao lost the scalpel but managed to loop his IV drip around Bond's neck. He started throttling him vigorously.

Bond reached back, grabbed the drip tube higher up, and wrapped it around Zao's neck. The scratchy pen monitoring Zao's heartbeat went into convulsions. They struggled together, each man trying to choke the other with the same drip tube. Bond let go and quickly clutched a gold bullet-shaped pendant dangling around Zao's neck. He pulled hard and smashed his fist into Zao's face. The force of the punch snapped the chain, leaving the pendant in Bond's hand.

The men fell apart. Zao pulled the tube from his neck, but Bond backfisted him and elbowed him in the stomach. Zao jumped for him, but Bond sidestepped and ran him into an opaque X-ray panel. Zao's head crashed through an X ray of himself and was pinned there, sparks flying around him.

"Answer the question. Who wanted you out?" Bond spat.

Zao made a superhuman effort to pull himself out of the panel and slammed into Bond's chest. Bond fell back, giving his opponent the time to go for the gun underneath the MRI. He snapped it up and aimed at Bond. Bond instinctively grabbed and hurled an isopropyl-alcohol bottle at the switch on the MRI. The bottle shattered and the liquid went everywhere. The machine's ultrastrong magnet activated and pinned Zao's gun hand to it. The killer dived out of the way as knives, scalpels, and hypodermics flew at the machine, narrowly missing him. Bond charged for the gun, but Zao toppled the broken and sparking mobile light into the pool of medicinal alcohol. Flames immediately shot up and set the bed on fire.

Bond switched off the MRI machine—the Walther dropped into his hand and all the knives and scalpels fell to the floor. He turned in time to dodge the burning bed that Zao rammed towards him. Bond took aim and tried to fire, but at that moment a medic stepped into the room. Zao grabbed the man and used him for cover as he moved for the door. Then he thrust the frightened medic at Bond and ran off down the corridor.

Bond opened his fist. The bullet pendant was still there. He pocketed it and ran after the terrorist.

At precisely the instant that Bond had made his way into the prohibited area, Jinx was having a consultation with Dr. Alvarez in the clinic director's office. The doctor, a middle-aged Cuban with thick-rimmed glasses and a bushy moustache, read Jinx's notes as he wandered around the room. The light glowed from his computer screen. Jinx sat before his desk, awaiting his pronouncement. She scanned the room and couldn't help admiring the various expensive pieces of art the doctor had collected. A Picasso and a Degas adorned the walls, and on a shelf was a glass case containing an opened, jewel-encrusted Fabergé egg. Beneath that she found what she was looking for—the safe that sat on the floor beneath the bookshelf.

"So, you are here to have DNA replacement therapy," Alvarez said.

"That's right," she replied.

"Let me explain the two phases. First, we kill off your bone marrow and wipe the DNA slate clean. A blank canvas, if you will." The doctor gave her a sick grin and continued. "Phase two is the introduction of new DNA harvested from healthy donors—orphans, runaways, people that won't be missed. I like to think of myself as an artist and this is when I . . . create. Be it a new ethnic group or just . . . bodily enhancements." He stepped behind her and rested his hands on her shoulders. "It is a painful process, I'm afraid. But all great art is. I will certainly enjoy working on you."

Jinx involuntarily shivered. She reached into a pocket on her dress and pulled out a cheque. The doctor smiled again and took it from her. He moved around to his chair behind the desk and examined the cheque, which was drawn from the Bank of the Cayman Islands. Suddenly a small round hole appeared in the centre of the cheque, accompanied by a low *fwip* sound. Alvarez stared at the hole in confusion, then down at his chest. Blood spread across his shirt. He looked at Jinx and saw that she was pointing a smoking, silenced Browning 9mm at him.

"Of course most artists are only appreciated after they're dead," she said. She fired again, this time through the doctor's skull. He fell back into the chair with a frozen expression of disbelief on his face. Jinx stood, leaned over the desk, and retrieved the cheque and notes. She picked up a cigarette lighter from the desk, flicked it on, and set fire to the pieces of paper. She let them burn in an ashtray as she walked around the desk to examine the doctor's computer. She typed a few commands and brought up a screen.

It was Zao's original face. A legend flashed: "Phase One Completed."

Jinx nodded to herself then typed more commands. The image disappeared and was replaced by a computer-generated image of Alvarez's safe. She punched some numbers and a screen queried: "Use combination in memory?" Jinx hit the *Y* button and the real safe opened.

This is almost too good to be true, she thought.

She shut down the computer and then moved to the

safe. Opening it wide, she rummaged through some papers and found the computer backup disk she was looking for. She lifted the hem of her dress, exposing a pouch fastened to her thigh. She placed the disk in the pouch and removed an explosive charge. Jinx stood, opened two filing cabinet drawers, pulled out some random files, and tossed them around the room. She manipulated some buttons on the object and the LED on top of it displayed the numbers 1:00. Jinx positioned the explosive charge amongst the pile of papers and pushed the last button. The timer began to count down from one minute.

Jinx immediately left the doctor's office as bells rang out through the building. The fire in Zao's room had set off an alarm, triggering escape lights and sprinklers. Several patients, pale and unfinished like Zao, shuffled along the corridor with drips attached. She peered through the swarm of bizarre figures and suddenly saw a familiar face at the end of the hall.

It was James Bond. Their eyes met and he ran towards her, still holding his Walther.

"James!" she exclaimed, abandoning her purposeful manner to become a wide-eyed innocent. "What's happening? Why do you have a gun?"

"You've got to get out!" he shouted.

Bond suddenly caught sight of Zao at the end of the corridor behind Jinx. There was a flash of his reptilian eyes as he recognised Bond, then he dived into the doctor's office.

"Now!" Bond shouted at Jinx, then he raced off after Zao.

"James—" Jinx tried to say, but he was gone. She

frowned, as part of her wanted to warn him—but it was too late. She shrugged and moved on.

Bond burst into Alvarez's office just in time to see Zao leaping from the broken window behind the desk. Bond ran across to the window, crouched, and aimed— just as Jinx's timer hit zero.

The desk protected Bond from the full force of the explosion. As it was, he was thrown against the wall. A section of the ceiling above the window collapsed, blocking his escape route. The room filled with smoke as the debris caught fire. Only then did Bond take in his surroundings. He saw the dead doctor on the floor, the open safe, the burning papers. . . .

He attempted to lift the debris in front of the window, but it was no use. The fire was raging between him and the office door. He was trapped.

Frantic, he looked around, found the doctor's lab coat, and used it as a shield. A wheeled trolley containing a nitrogen cylinder sat in the corner. Bond leapt for it and dragged it over broken glass. He pointed the cylinder at a blank wall eight feet away. He then pulled a fire extinguisher off the wall and used it to hammer the valve off the nitrogen cylinder. Nitrogen shot out, propelling the trolley forward until it exploded. Bond dived into the smoke, through the hole, and landed in the other room. From there he ran back into the corridor and made his way up to the quad. He looked out the window and saw Zao down below on the clinic landing pad, knocking down a guard who was protecting an ambulance helicopter. Zao forced his way into the chopper and threw the pilot out onto the tarmac. The rotors started turning and the helicopter began to rise.

Then Bond saw Jinx running up the sloping battlement at full tilt, firing a pistol. She was apparently aiming at Zao, but the helicopter was ascending too quickly. Zao leaned out of the chopper and fired a machine gun back at her but failed to hit his target. Jinx continued to shoot, but her clip clicked empty. The helicopter got away.

Two armed guards approached Jinx. She dropped her gun and then unzipped her dress. It fell to her feet, revealing the sexy bikini she had worn the day before. She kicked off her heels and then raised her arms above her head in a classic surrender. The two guards were beguiled. Jinx looked up and saw Bond watching her. She gave him a look of wry acknowledgement and then she let herself fall backwards into thin air.

A two-hundred-foot back dive.

Bond watched with amazement as her figure sailed downward in beautiful formation and hit the water like a knife. A boat appeared out of nowhere, obviously poised to pick her up. She surfaced and clambered aboard. Bond was unable to see who else was on the boat as it shot off towards Cuba, cutting a white wake through the blue.

Bond smiled in simple admiration.

He turned from the window and fished Zao's bullet pendant out of his pocket. He could feel that it was hollow, so he unscrewed the base and turned it over.

Diamonds spilled out into his palm.

9

A Man Called Graves

Raoul focused the small 1950s optical machine so that it projected a chromatic display of one of the diamond's innermost colours onto a card. He looked through a microscope and studied the pattern.

Bond stood nearby and reflected on the events of the past twenty-four hours. In his disguise as a clinic orderly, he had managed to gain passage from Isla Organos back to Cuba with no problem. The boat had been crowded with staff and patients, but it was apparent that some people hadn't made it. By the time emergency services arrived at the scene, the clinic had completely burned down.

Bond had searched for Jinx at the hotel, but as he expected, there was no sign of her. He had even made enquiries at the quay, but the guard told him that he hadn't seen her. The boat she had gotten on must have sped to another part of the island, where she had disembarked and disappeared.

Now Bond was back in Raoul's study in the Havana cigar factory. He was confident that he could trust the Cuban and had asked him to analyse the diamonds that were in Zao's pendant.

"Hmm," Raoul said. "Beautiful . . . but illegal. The chemical composition shows this is from Sierra Leone. They're conflict diamonds. Since the UN put an embargo on them, they're worthless."

Raoul gestured to the microscope and Bond looked through it. He was no expert in identifying the gems, but he knew a little about points and how diamonds were cut and polished.

"Makes sense," he said, admiring the craftsmanship. "Zao was involved in trading them once before. Look at this; there's some kind of marking. It looks like *GG*."

He moved away and allowed Raoul to look.

"Ah, yes," Raoul concurred. He, too, could see the tiny GG logo etched into one of the facets, invisible to the naked eye. "My mistake. These diamonds *are* legal. They are from Graves's mine in Iceland. That's his laser signature."

"Graves?"

"Gustav Graves made a huge find up there a year or so ago."

"I'm not familiar with him."

Raoul looked at Bond with surprise. "Where have you been?"

"Humour me. Who is he?"

"Very rich industrialist who likes publicity. Came from nowhere and was an overnight success. He's working on some kind of space technology but makes his living with the diamond mine. Extraordinary specimens, I must say."

Bond raised an eyebrow. "And yet they're identical to conflict diamonds? What an amazing coincidence."

Miss Moneypenny was hoping that M would bring up 007's whereabouts during the heated discussion with the Americans.

MI6's executive assistant sat in M's outer office with her ear to the intercom, eavesdropping on what was going on within the inner office. Normally she minded her own business when M was dealing with problems behind closed doors, but Moneypenny was certain that right then they were discussing James Bond.

Charles Robinson surprised her by asking, "Tuned in to an interesting station?" He was standing in the doorway, having appeared without her noticing.

Moneypenny jumped and switched off the intercom. "All I got was a storm warning," she said, embarrassed.

Robinson understood her meaning and nodded. He passed through to the padded door and entered the inner sanctum.

M was on a video link with the NSA agent Falco and it was obvious that the American was angry.

"Look," Falco said, "I don't understand why you couldn't stick to the deal. Keep him under lock and key."

"Are you implying that I had a hand in his escape, Mr. Falco?" M asked.

"Well, he got away real fast!"

"It's what he's *trained* to do."

"I want to show you something," Falco said. "This is security-camera footage that we obtained from the

Alvarez Clinic in Cuba. Take a look at this."

The screen filled with images of Bond entering the lobby of the clinic, pushing Krug in the wheelchair. This was followed by a shot of Bond running down a smoke-filled corridor, gun in hand. A clip from the BBC came next, showing an aerial view of the blazing clinic. Patients and staff were running about in a panic.

M was genuinely shocked. Falco came back on the screen and said, "Bond's out of control. He arrives in Havana, and the next thing we know, a clinic is burning down. Now we've heard he's headed for London. If you can't put your house in order, we'll do it for you."

Falco ended the transmission without saying good-bye.

M looked at Robinson with a grim face.

"Every point of entry is an alert," he said, anticipating her orders. "Bond wouldn't come back here. He'd be out of his mind."

The British Airways 747 jumbo jet banked eastward and began its descent over London. It was nearly time for James Bond to make his move. He finished the last few sentences of the article in the *High Life* magazine he was reading and then took a long look at the cover photo. The lead story was about the exploits of action man/businessman Gustav Graves. An Argentinean orphan with dual British citizenship, he had only recently come into the international spotlight as a multimillionaire who was funding the development of secretive space programs. He had his hand in a number of businesses, but Bond was interested in him because of the diamonds. Apparently Graves owned a mine and diamond-processing centre in Iceland. The profile in the magazine described him as a philanthropist who gave freely to various charities and, though not yet thirty years old, something of a financial genius. He was also an adventurer. Graves enjoyed ballooning, mountaineering, and was a fencing champion. The photos featured a young man of serious good looks, dark hair, and blue eyes. He might have been a male model.

As Bond was one of only four passengers in the first-class cabin, he had almost the full attention of the pretty flight attendant who had served him a martini half an hour earlier. She began to walk along the aisle, preparing the cabin for landing, and stopped beside Bond's seat to take his glass. The plane shook a little from turbulence, and she reached for the back of a seat to steady herself.

"Lucky I asked for it shaken," Bond said, handing the empty glass to her. She smiled and asked him to bring his seat upright, then moved aft, gathering empty glasses from other passengers.

"Beds back to vertical, please," she announced. "We're coming in to land."

She turned back to get another glimpse of the handsome man who liked martinis and was surprised to see that his seat was empty. She moved back to it and saw that the copy of *High Life* lay in his place.

As the plane lined up with the river for its final approach, the massive nosewheel emerged from its resting place beneath the fuselage. James Bond was holding on to the strut. The wind buffeted him but he enjoyed the view—Big Ben on one side of the river, the MI6 building on the other.

It was a trick he had tried only once before, and that had been on a smaller plane. The mechanics were the same, however. The difficult part was getting from the cabin to the inner fuselage. Few people other than airline personnel knew about the compartment in the galley that allowed emergency access to the bowels of the plane. When the flight attendant wasn't looking, he had slipped into the galley, opened the trapdoor, and down he went.

Thankfully, the weather was pleasant and warm.

The plane touched down at Heathrow without any problems. As soon as the aircraft had taxied off the runway and pulled into the gate, Bond undid the belt and jumped off the wheel strut. No one saw him. He nonchalantly walked away from the plane as the baggage handlers showed up to unload.

Londoners were used to huge crowds in front of Buckingham Palace. On this particular afternoon, TV cameras, newspaper photographers, and a throng of journalists had joined the enormous crowd of spectators and tourists gathered across from the Queen Victoria Memorial to await the arrival of one man. The problem was that he was late. Traffic was backed up in all directions and people were becoming impatient and restless.

James Bond had lost himself in the crowd. He, too, was waiting for the celebrity's imminent arrival, but his eyes were focused on the attractive young woman who was part of the man's press team. She was smartly dressed, in her twenties, and had blonde hair and an easy athleticism that was obvious despite her professional attitude.

A reporter loudly proclaimed, "Looks like he's not going to make it."

The blonde answered him, loud enough for all to hear. "Oh, you should know better than to count Gustav out." She pulled out a mobile, punched some numbers, and talked quietly into it. After a few moments she shut the mobile and made a loud announcement to the crowd. She was obviously used to raising her voice in front of large groups of people.

"I'm sure Gustav will be along very soon. I know he wouldn't be late for the Queen." She looked up to the skies and smiled. "In fact, there he is now." She pointed and shielded her eyes from the bright sun. Everyone followed suit.

A man had just jumped from a small aircraft. Within seconds, a Union Jack parachute opened and he floated dramatically down into Green Park. Newscasters directed their television cameras at him while photographers snapped away.

Gustav Graves landed with finesse and pulled off his chute. The crowd applauded as he walked across to a waiting limousine and reporters suddenly rushed at him. Bond coolly regarded the whole media event. Graves certainly had style and he knew how to turn it into a photo opportunity.

"What a wonderful day to become a knight!" he said to the cameras. Everyone laughed.

The young woman joined him, deftly creating a small space for Graves in the crowd to give the cameras a better view.

"And *will* you be using your title?"

Graves shook his head and waved the question away. "You know me. I'm proud of my adopted nation, but I'd never stand on ceremony." He had a refined, very English accent.

"After an entrance like that, you can't be surprised you've been called a self-publicising adrenaline junkie?"

"I prefer the term 'adventurer.'"

"Mr. Graves. What is it we've been hearing about rockets being launched, this Icarus Space Program? What's the big secret?"

Graves smiled. "It's not a secret, it's a surprise. Believe me, all will soon be revealed."

"You seem to work nonstop. Is it true that you don't need sleep?"

Graves waved his hand, dismissing the question. "You only get one shot at life—why squander it on sleep? While others doze I am thinking of ways to improve the world."

One reporter tried to needle him. "Critics say you're just purporting to love this country to fool people into liking you. All part of a carefully manufactured image."

Graves looked at the man coolly. "'Purporting'? I can assure you I haven't purported in years." The crowd laughed. "I want my adopted nation to be proud of me and proud of itself."

"Is that also why you're trying for a place on the British Olympic fencing team? We hear you've been training furiously."

"Oh, I never get furious. As they say in fencing, 'What's the point?'"

More laughter. Graves waved good-bye and turned to get into the car. The young woman held up her hands to keep the reporters back.

"Thank you, everyone!" she shouted. "You'll forgive Gustav for not keeping Her Majesty waiting." She nodded to three policemen, who took over handling the crowd as the car moved away and passed through the palace gates.

Bond stepped away from the crowd, reflecting on what he had just seen and heard. The man was an exhibitionist, an extrovert, and an egotist—three traits that Bond didn't care for. For such a man to come out of apparently nowhere struck him as highly questionable.

Bond looked forward to meeting Graves.

10

Flashing Blades at St. James's

The long-standing London gentlemen's club off St. James's Street was typical of such Regency establishments that had always provided safe haven for their members. Since the eighteenth century, gentlemen had gathered here to dine and read in silence, to gossip and plot, and to take advantage of the well-stocked, cavernous wine cellars. Gambling and cardplaying was an accepted part of polite English society so long as it took place within a gentleman's club, and many establishments went beyond this to offer other chances for sport.

The fencing hall, or "salle," has been a habitat of the wellborn sportsman since the eighteenth century. Fencing, a pursuit that combines aggression and grace, is perfectly suited the needs of elegant gentlemen.

Bond climbed the steps to the club; he thought it was safe for him to appear there. He knew of no one else from the Service who was now a member, and it was doubtful that the Immigration Service kept watch on these discreet doors. His membership was a long-standing one, and he was able to slip down to the changing rooms without delay. Modernisation comes slowly to such establishments, but this club had managed to encompass modern plumbing and the introduction of women members without noticeably destroying the charms of the elegant, slightly faded fencing floor.

Bond went straight to the dressing room and changed into his fencing whites. It had been a while since he had done any fencing, but he kept telling himself that it was just like riding a bike.

When he was ready, he walked down to the cavernous hall. The noise and energy of the matches being played was all but palpable.

Bond spotted Graves immediately and saw that there was an audience of nearly a dozen people. The hall was divided into several duelling floors and was decorated with massive display cases full of antique weapons from various cultures around the world.

The bout was in full swing. Two figures, dressed in full fencing regalia and masks, were fighting with intense speed and skill. The players were connected to "electronic referees" by wires that extended from their tunics. Graves's opponent was a woman, and she was a startlingly good fencer. At the moment she was aggressively forcing Graves to back up, putting him on the defensive. However, Graves managed to parry the woman's sword with a swift manoeuvre called *in quartata,* a counterattack made with a quarter turn to the inside, concealing the front but exposing the back. This allowed him to pull away and regain a position in the centre of the court. Before they could continue the bout, the electronic referees lit up and sounded the end of the match. Graves had won, but only by a little.

Graves removed his mask and was all smiles. The other mask came off and a shock of blond hair tumbled down. It was the woman Bond had seen with Graves outside Buckingham Palace.

As the pair slapped hands and moved off the floor for a breather, Bond noticed the club's lovely fencing coach standing in the corner. She was tall and thin, had long black hair, and appeared to be in her thirties. She was also dressed for fencing, but the laces on her corset were still undone.

He approached her. "Verity?"

"Yes?"

"James Bond. Your lesson."

"Oh, right. I've been expecting you." She looked him up and down. A hint of a smile indicated that she liked what she saw. "You can tell so much about a man from the way he handles his weapon."

"Oh, I'm sure there's lots you can teach me," he replied.

She turned her back to him. "Do me up, will you?"

"My pleasure." He pulled the laces tight and she winced. "I don't believe I've seen you here before."

"That makes two of us. I'm here every day. Where have you been?"

"I've been away. Do you fence with other members?"

"Sure. Watch and learn. The finest blade in the club's right there."

"Gustav Graves? Have you ever crossed swords with him?" Bond asked.

"He only likes to bet," she said, shaking her head.

"What about his opponent? Who's she?"

"Miranda Frost, his publicist. A difficult girl to lick. Believe me, I've tried. Won the gold at Sydney."

Bond pulled the laces tighter. His memory stirred, he added, "By default, I seem to remember . . . ?"

Verity exhaled to accommodate the fit. "Yeah, after the one who beat her OD'd on steroids. Miranda *deserved* her gold."

"And now she's teaching Graves how to win one."

"He has trouble finding partners. He's taken so much off the other members that he's scared them off."

Bond thought about this a moment and asked, "Could you engineer an introduction?"

Verity looked at him as if he were crazy. "Without a lesson from me? Are you sure you're ready for that?"

Bond smiled winningly and shrugged.

They went over to where Graves was towelling the back of his neck.

"Mr. Graves, one of our members wants to meet you," Verity said. Graves looked up and smiled at him curiously. "And perhaps try a bout with you," she added.

"Bond. James Bond." He extended his hand, but Graves made no move to accept it. His hands were full—mask in one, sword in the other. Miranda overheard and stepped next to them.

"Have we met before?" Graves asked.

"I think I'd remember," Bond replied.

"Of course you would. My mistake. Are you a gambling man, Mr. Bond?"

"When the odds are right . . ."

"Surely you could risk a thousand against me?"

Bond looked at Miranda. She gave him a cold stare

96

as she disconnected herself from the scoring equipment and handed him the wire. Bond connected it to the back of his protective gear, then attached a wire from his sword's hilt to the wrist of his jacket.

"Thank you . . ." he said, awaiting her name.

"Frost. Miranda Frost. And I heard. You're Bond." She was well-spoken but cold as ice. He smiled, but she didn't return it.

"Be careful of Miss Frost, Mr. Bond," Graves said. "She might bruise more than your ego."

"Is your lesson with her over?" he asked Graves, taunting him a bit.

The man eyed Bond solemnly. "Best-of-three hits?"

Bond nodded.

The two men put on their masks and stepped onto the duelling floor. They assumed the en garde position, waited for the start, and engaged. Miranda and Verity watched with interest as the fencers moved slowly, warily, sizing each other up. Then the assaults began. A lunge, parry, and a feint—and Bond was tagged by Graves's tip. A light on the electric referee signalled a hit, accompanied by a loud zap. Verity shook her head to herself. She obviously thought Bond was outclassed.

Next point. The men engaged and Graves swiftly performed a *froissement,* an attack that displaced the opponent's blade with a strong grazing action. He scored a hit.

"Two nil," Graves said. "I win. Perhaps you're not at ease with the electronic scoring, Mr. Bond. Too . . . civilised for you?"

"Oh, I'll give it another go," Bond replied nonchalantly.

"Let's up the wager, then, shall we? How much can you afford?"

Bond kept his cool. "How much can you?" He pulled one of Zao's diamonds out of his pocket and tossed it to Graves. "Why not play for this? I picked it up in Cuba."

Graves removed his mask and took a closer look at the gem. Bond detected a slight flash of anger in the man's eyes.

"My, they do get around," Graves said with control. "But then, diamonds are for everyone." He tossed the diamond back and locked eyes with Bond. "A particularly brilliant specimen. Completely flawless."

"And chemically identical to African blood diamonds."

Graves raised his blade and said, "You're about to lose something very precious." He lowered his mask and assumed en garde. Bond did the same and the bout began again. Graves immediately engaged Bond's blade with an envelopment, a manoeuvre that swept the opponent's sword through a full circle. Bond, however, counterparried, a move made in the opposite line to the attack. Doing so knocked Graves's sword away and Bond quickly lunged and scored a hit.

Graves was surprised, as was everyone else.

Bond shrugged, self-deprecating. "Pure luck. Like your diamond find."

This provoked Graves into a reckless lunge that let Bond slash Graves's wire—and his wrist.

"Oh, sorry about that," Bond said. "Accidents will happen."

Graves threw off his mask and glared at him, sucking blood from the cut. The damaged wire was making the scoreboard *zap, zap, zap* on Graves's side, infuriating him.

"You want to continue?" Bond asked.

"Of course I want to bloody continue!" Calming down fast, he severed the remnants of the wire, ripped open his lamé, and strode to two large ceremonial sabre swords on the wall. "But if we're upping the wager, let's up the weapons!" He then removed his tunic, revealing a T-shirt underneath. "Why don't we do this the old-fashioned way?" He took down the sabres. "First blood drawn from the torso." He said it as a given, then tossed one of the sabres to Bond.

Bond removed his jacket, too. Then he discarded the mask, throwing it down next to Graves's. He nodded at the masks and said, "They were slipping anyway."

The fight commenced "dry," that is, without the electronic judging aids. Bond found the sabre awkward and unwieldy.

Graves advanced with ferocity and surprised Bond with a cross, a movement in which the attacker crossed one leg over the other in order to change directions midstride. The back-and-forth play of the blades in a fencing match is called "conversation," and Bond thought to himself that this particular one was more like a heated argument. The sabres clashed and slashed viciously, and Bond was coming off worse. Graves had him on the defensive, backing him against a display case. Graves attempted a thrust, which might very well have skewered Bond had he not spun out of the way. The sword broke the glass on the case, scattering slivers all over the floor.

This didn't stop them. Graves kept after his adversary, but Bond performed successful parries and attempted to push his opponent's blade aside with a "press" manoeuvre. As soon as there was an opening, Bond directly attacked Graves, but succeeded only in prodding him.

A murmur had begun spreading around the hall as other people realised that something serious was happening. They all stopped to watch.

After nearly a minute of fierce engagement, Graves performed a *balestra,* a forward jump followed by a lunge, but Bond somehow anticipated it and parried out of the way. Graves crashed into one of the massive display cases, knocking it loose. Broadswords, maces, battle-axes, and nearly every other conceivable type of bladed weapon fell in a rain of steel.

Now having completely lost his composure, Graves picked up a broadsword and threw the sabre aside. He was playing for keeps now, and Bond knew it, but he wasn't sure if the spectators understood how earnest the fight had become. Graves attacked with the new sword, and for a few moments Bond's sabre was outclassed. Graves cornered Bond again near another display case and swung the broadsword in a dangerous arc that might have lopped off his opponent's head. Bond ducked and grabbed one of the other broadswords that lay at his feet. He dropped, rolled, and leapt to his feet before Graves's sword came crashing down.

Bond tried a feint but failed as Graves counterattacked and pushed him against the double doors that led to an elegant courtyard. He fell through and the fight spilled into the sunlight. Graves raised the broadsword high and brought it down hard. Bond rolled and jumped up, just in time to parry another blow. The two men continued to spar vigorously around a flowing, ornate fountain in the middle of the courtyard.

Graves suddenly advanced in double time and performed a *coulé*, an attack that slid his sword along his opponent's blade. The sword slashed Bond's torso, drawing blood. Bond parried and nicked the skin on Graves's ear. The man's eyes flared. Bond could see that Graves was crazy with anger. He didn't just want to win the bet—he wanted to kill.

They fought on, with Graves backing Bond to the fountain, punching with his hilt. But Bond produced a flurry that cut Graves's leg, throwing him off balance. The man tried to prevent the fall with his sword, but succeeded only in breaking the blade. Graves splashed backwards through the water and ended up with his back against the statue in the centre of the fountain. Bond was immediately there, his blade pressed to Graves's throat, just as Graves's own broken blade positioned against Bond's.

Suddenly a sword hurtled between the two men's faces, digging into the statue. The incredible speed and accuracy of the move shook them from their battle. They looked along the blade to the wielder of the sword.

"That's enough!" Miranda cried. She glared at Bond intently. After a beat, Bond backed away from Graves.

"Gustav, you forget yourself," she scolded.

Graves became aware of the people all around, the faces at the windows, and the spectacle he had made of himself. Bond offered his hand, and the mask of good humour slid back over the man's face. He allowed Bond to help him out of the fountain.

"Just a little sport, Miranda," he said. She handed

him a towel. "Mr. Bond, you fought like a true Englishman. You'll take a cheque?"

"From you?" Bond asked. "Of course."

As they headed back to the hall, Miranda attempted to touch Graves's wound, but he brushed her aside.

"You're a rare challenge, Mr. Bond," Graves said as they walked. "I'm putting on a little scientific demonstration in Iceland this weekend. Perhaps you've heard of it. Icarus. I hope you'll come along. I have lots of fun and games planned. And worthy opponents are so hard to find." He turned to Miranda. She knew it was her cue to produce the chequebook. Graves took it and wrote one out to Bond.

"Make the arrangements for Mr. Bond to visit us in Iceland, would you?" he told her as he handed the book back.

"Once I've smoothed things over with the club," she replied, her displeasure not well hidden.

"What would I do without you?" he quipped, knowing that she would take care of everything without much fuss.

He strode off, leaving Miranda face-to-face with Bond. She ripped out the cheque and handed it over.

"Can I expect the pleasure of you in Iceland?" Bond asked smoothly.

She remained as icy as ever. "I'm afraid you'll never have that pleasure, Mr. Bond." With that, she stormed off after Graves. Bond watched her go and wondered what it was that made her such an ice maiden.

A concierge appeared among the members of staff who had begun bearing away the damaged furniture and artwork. "Someone left this for you, sir," he said, handing Bond an envelope. As he walked away, the man eyed the destruction and muttered, "Place needed re-decorating anyway."

Bond weighed the envelope in his hand, recognising the paper stock. He tore it open and out dropped a distinctive iron key.

11

Reinstated

Bond walked to Whitehall and then skirted southwest towards Westminster Bridge, avoiding the pedestrians that surrounded him. He rarely travelled on foot in this fashion, but he had no other choice. He couldn't very well go to his flat, as it was probably being watched. The sensible thing would be to see the game through as it unfolded. *They* had played a trump card. He either had to make a countermove or to obey the rules and follow procedure. Bond decided on the latter. He took a turn and made his way into the shadows. He carefully looked around to make sure no one had seen him, and then he approached the dark, iron door underneath an arch. Bond took the heavy key out of his pocket and used it to unlock the rusty door. It squeaked unmercifully when he opened it. He stepped inside and shut the door with loud *clang*.

He stood for a moment to allow his eyes to get used to the dark. When he could see fairly well, he moved forward and came upon a metal spiral staircase leading down. Bond descended slowly until he came to a dusty, disused underground train platform. An otherworldly subterranean network existed beneath London. Since the underground was the oldest subway system in the world, it was only natural that stations, tunnels, and entire lines had gone out of commission over the last century. Lords, British Museum, and Aldwych are just some of those haunting "lost" stations of London. Some had never even opened, like the Bull and Bush station near Hampstead Heath. Some had been shut when lines were modernised, such as City Road. Others were abandoned as hopeless cases, such as South Kentish Town, which had attracted few passengers.

Sometimes whole lines disappeared, including the original route under the Thames. Particularly mysterious are two Piccadilly line stations, Brompton Road and Down Street, between Berkeley Street and Piccadilly. Brompton Road had been used by the War Office during World War II, and rumours had flown around in wartime that Winston Churchill was frequently seen crossing Green Park between Whitehall and Down Street. Rumours and myths surround many "ghost stations," and Bond knew of many secret tunnels and depots. He had never been down these stairs, but all Double-O agents knew what was there. He saw a light at the far end and walked towards it.

M was waiting for him in the open doorway.

Bond handed her the key and said rather coldly, "Your calling card." She took it but said nothing. Bond looked around the dark station and remarked, "I heard about this place, but I never thought I'd find myself here."

"Some things are best kept underground," she said softly.

"An abandoned station for abandoned agents?"

M gestured for him to go through the door. They walked together past faded advertising placards from the 1950s. The air was cold and damp, and for a moment Bond was reminded of his time in the North Korean prison cell. They turned a corner and came to a decrepit, old-fashioned firing range where tattered paper targets dangled on wires.

M brushed a stool off with a handkerchief and sat down. She indicated another one for Bond, and he sat across from her.

"So what have you got on Graves?" she asked.

Bond blinked. "You burn me and now you want my help . . ."

"What did you expect, an apology?"

"I know, I know—you'll do whatever it takes to get the job done."

"Just like you."

"The difference is, I won't compromise."

"Well, I don't have the luxury of seeing things as black and white." She sighed, trying a different approach. "While you were away, the world changed."

"Not for me." He narrowed his eyes at her. "You're suspicious of Graves or I wouldn't be here now. What do *you* have?"

"Nothing beyond the official biography. Orphan working in Argentinean diamond mine, learns engineering. Makes a huge find in Iceland—and gives half of it to charity."

"From nothing to too good to be true—in no time at all." He shook his head. "And his demonstration this weekend? What about that?"

M brushed it off. "Probably just another publicity stunt. Using space technology to feed the world. Now, what about this Cuban clinic? You tracked Zao there, yes?"

He nodded. "Gene therapy. New identities, courtesy of DNA transplants."

"The so-called Beauty Parlour. We'd heard rumours of such a place. I didn't think it really existed."

Bond reached into his pocket and produced a few diamonds. M's eyes widened.

"Zao got away, but he left these. *All* from Gustav Graves's mine. I think it's a front for laundering African conflict diamonds."

She frowned. "We need to tread carefully. Graves is politically connected."

"Lucky I'm on the outside then," Bond said ironically.

"It seems you've become useful again."

"Then maybe it's time you let me get on with my job."

MI6 headquarters at Vauxhall Cross was always a bee-hive of activity during daylight hours, but at night it became astonishingly quiet. Bond sat in his private office, a place where he spent as little time as possible, cleaning his Walther by the light of a desk lamp and accompanied by a half-full tumbler of whisky. His jacket was draped around the chair.

The office hadn't changed much over the years. It was sparsely furnished and rather lifeless, with no indication that its occupant was a man with any particular interests. There were no framed photographs of the family, no personal additions to the simple items on his desk, and no framed prints or posters on the walls. The only grim testament to the nature of his profession, a 4.2 calibre gold bullet engraved with the number "007," was out of sight in a desk drawer. The room was utterly impersonal. Bond had always liked it that way.

He took a swig of Scotch. He told himself that he should go home to his flat off the King's Road and get some sleep. He was tired. He was—

The sound of muffled gunfire sent a jolt of adrenaline through his body. It came from somewhere above. M's floor?

Alert now, Bond quickly assembled his gun, loaded a magazine, stood, and moved to the door. He peered out into the darkened corridor, but it was silent on his floor. He sprinted quietly past the lift towards the stairs. Bond went into the stairwell, raced up a flight, and listened at the door on the next level.

Too quiet.

He kicked the door open and saw one of the security guards—dead, lying in a pool of blood. Two shadows flitted across the floor. Bond swung out of the stairwell and fired two rounds. One of the intruders fell back and crashed into the wall of a cubicle. The entire structure fell with a clamour. The second man jerked violently and immediately went down. Bond listened, looked in all directions, then proceeded towards the bodies. He didn't recognise them. They appeared to be in their thirties and were dressed in black. One had a Smith & Wesson in his hand.

Bond thought he heard a muffled scream coming

from M's office. Catlike, he moved to the door, put his ear to it, then burst it open.

Another black-clad gunman had a terrified Moneypenny in his grip, his hand covering her mouth. She wrenched her face free and shouted, "James, help me!" The man thrust the barrel of a Smith & Wesson into her temple.

Bond set his jaw and raised the Walther. He took a careful bead on the target and squeezed the trigger. A perfect shot. The man released Moneypenny, dropped the gun, and fell back in a crumpled heap. Bond moved towards Moneypenny, but she looked past him, her eyes widening.

Bond whirled around to see another dark figure with a gun. The Walther came up, just as the man moved into the light. It was Robinson. Bond breathed a sigh of relief—good thing he hadn't pulled the trigger. Robinson put a finger to his lips and pointed to M's door. Before Bond could react, Robinson crossed the room and kicked the door open. He and Bond rushed into the inner office only to find it empty.

"Come on," Robinson said.

Bond followed him out into the corridor. There was a bit of noise near the lifts. They picked up their pace and got within thirty feet of the area when a shot rang out. Robinson cried, spun, and fell back into a chart tacked onto Peg-Board. He left a smear of blood on it as he sank to the floor.

Bond used a cubicle wall for cover to peek around to the lifts. There was another assassin holding M in front of him. The lift was on its way. The digital readout showed that it had two floors to go. If the doors opened and they got on, he would lose the chance to save her.

"Come on, if you have the guts," the man called.

One more floor and the lift would be there. Bond hesitated, then aimed the gun at the villain's head. M was in the way. He couldn't get a clean shot. There was only one thing to do.

The lift doors opened. Bond squeezed the trigger. The bullet went straight into M's shoulder, passed through her and into the assailant's heart. The man released M and looked down at the hole in his chest. With anger and disbelief on his face, he raised his gun to fire at Bond.

The Walther barked again. This time the intruder slammed backwards into the open lift.

All was still for a moment. Then suddenly the man decelerated, levitating "forward" to land on his feet, as if he were a piece of film being run backwards. Then, without explanation, he stood there frozen, reenacting his reaction when Bond had shot him.

"My commiserations, Double-O Zero. But I'm afraid shooting the boss counts as a fail."

Bond sighed as Q walked through the back wall of the corridor, which flickered and revealed a wire-frame structure behind it. Beyond that, the rest of the Virtual Shooting Range Chamber materialised and all remnants of the MI6 illusion disappeared as Q stepped into the scene. He could barely contain his glee at his simulator's defeat of Bond.

Bond removed his headset and moved off the motion-sensing floorplate.

"Check the replay, Q, you'll find he's dead and she's only got a flesh wound."

"There's always an excuse, isn't there."

Bond rolled his eyes and holstered his gun. He

walked towards the chamber's exit and said, "The whisky tasted pretty good, but I'll take the old firing range any day, Quartermaster."

Q was hot on his heels. "Well, it's called the *future,* so get used to it!"

They went through the door and into another part of the underground station. Bond was amazed by the amount of space that SIS owned away from the main headquarters. He had never known that Q Branch kept another experimental workshop in this part of London. Perhaps he really *had* been away too long.

"You know, this has been in use since wartime," Q commented proudly.

"One of the few places in central London where it was possible to sleep without being disturbed by bombing. I enjoy the quiet down here, too. I can work in *peace.*"

The place was littered with old and new gadgets. Bond felt a bit of nostalgia when he saw some of the antiquated items—a jet pack hanging on a stand, a miniature rebreather, a grappling-hook gun, the old folding sniper's rifle and attaché case. There were bullet-ridden dummies with limbs missing piled in a corner as well as several shelving units with all manner of weaponry on them. A miniature gyro-copter, unused for years, sat gathering dust.

"So this is where they keep the old relics," Bond said.

He idly touched a button on the jet pack. It roared loudly, blasting the ground and blowing papers everywhere. Q pushed Bond away and switched it off before it actually started to rise.

"I'll have you know this is where our most cutting-edge technology is developed," Q grumbled.

But Bond had moved on. He fingered the old attaché case and found the hidden button that released the hidden dagger.

"Point taken," Bond said.

Q slipped on a pair of protective glasses, picked up a .357 Magnum, and pointed it just past Bond. Bond leapt out of the way as Q fired. The noise was tremendous. Bond looked to see what Q was firing at, but there was nothing. He walked in that direction and saw that a sheet of glass stood in the way—the bullet was smashed and stuck into it.

"One sheet of unbreakable glass, one standard-issue ring. Twist so and voilà!" Q said, holding up his right hand. He manipulated something on a ring he wore on his fourth finger. Bond heard a high-pitched noise and the glass began to vibrate. It suddenly shattered and fell to pieces. Q smiled gleefully, removed the ring, and handed it to Bond.

"It's really an ultra-high-frequency single-digit sonic agitator unit."

"You know, you're cleverer than you look," Bond said.

"Better than looking cleverer than you are." Q picked a watch off a table and handed it to Bond. "This'll be your twentieth, I believe."

"Doesn't time fly?"

"Yes, well, why don't you establish a record by actually returning this one? Now follow me, if you please."

Q started up a short flight of stairs to a tiled tube passage. Bond followed him until they arrived at another unused underground platform.

"Your new transportation." Q pressed a button on the

wall and a flatbed rail truck emerged from the darkness of the tunnel. In the half-light of the underground, it appeared to be completely empty.

Bond glanced at Q and back at the truck. "I'd heard about the budget cuts . . ."

Q stepped onto the truck and began walking around the outside edges, feasting his eyes on thin air. "It's the ultimate in British engineering."

"Maybe you've been down here too long, Q," Bond said, staring at him.

Q began to fiddle with a keyfob and Bond thought his eyes were playing tricks on him. Q's body distorted weirdly.

"You've got to be joking," Bond said to himself.

"As I learnt from my predecessor, Bond. I *never* joke about my work." He pressed another button on the key-fob and a shape began to materialise on the flatbed. First it was just a sea of swimming pixels, then it all came together to become a beautiful, muscular car.

"Aston Martin call it the Vanquish. We call it the Vanish," Q said.

It was astonishing.

"Adaptive camouflage," Q explained. "Tiny cameras on all sides project the image they see onto a light-emitting polymer skin on the *opposite* side. To the casual eye, it's as good as invisible. Of course, the usual panoply of refinements—ejector seat, torpedoes and"— he punched the keyfob and two powerful-looking guns unfolded from the car's flanks—"twelve-gauge target-seeking shotguns to hunt out moving objects."

"But how does it handle?" Bond asked.

Q made a face and replied, "It will reach one hundred and ninety miles per hour and can accelerate from a standstill to sixty-two miles per hour in less than five seconds. There's a six-litre V12 engine, six-speed manual transmission operated by an electrohydraulic gearshift without the use of a clutch pedal. With a flick of the steering-column-mounted paddle shifters, you can change gears in approximately two hundred and fifty milliseconds. That's about as fast as you can blink, Double-O Seven."

Q reached through the car window and pulled out a huge book that looked like the London phone directory. "Now. Why don't you acquaint yourself with the owner's manual. Should be able to shoot through it in a few hours."

He handed it to Bond. It was ridiculously heavy. Bond considered it, then glanced at the target-seeking guns. Q realised what Bond was thinking but was too late to stop him from lobbing the manual up ahead of the car. The guns whirred into life and blasted the book into smithereens. Tattered pages drifted down around them.

"It only took a few seconds, Q," Bond said.

"If only I could make *you* vanish," Q muttered.

As Q was giving Bond a guided tour of the underground Q Branch Extension, M was back in her office at the MI6 Vauxhall headquarters reviewing the files on Gustav Graves. She picked up the phone and summoned one of her newer and more promising agents. When she heard the knock on the door, M said, "Come."

When the two of them were alone, M grimly addressed the young agent. "Before you leave for your mission in Iceland, tell me what you know of James Bond."

The agent replied coolly and calmly. "A Double-O. A wild one—as I witnessed today. Will light the fuse on any explosive situation. Kill first, ask questions later. A danger to himself and others. A blunt instrument whose primary method is to provoke and confront. A womaniser."

"Well, you're going to be seeing a lot more of him in Iceland."

"With respect, a man like him could blow my cover."

"Only if he finds out who you are. Look, you volunteered for this operation, you did well tipping us off when Bond appeared—but in three months you've turned up next to nothing."

"Graves seems to be clean."

"Well, Bond thinks differently. So I'm going to let him do what you so ably described. Mix things up a little with Mr. Graves. And with you there, things won't be able to get out of hand."

She could see that the young agent wasn't happy about this. M continued, "While Bond may have been through a lot, one thing I'm sure hasn't changed is his desire for beautiful women. In your three years in cryptology, you managed to keep business and pleasure separate." She looked down at the agent's file. "You've not 'fraternised' with any of your fellow agents despite several advances."

"It would be foolish to get involved with someone within the community," Miranda Frost replied. "Especially James Bond."

12

The Ice Palace

The Aston Martin Vanquish cruised along nicely over a cliff-top road that traversed the edges of Vatnajökull, the largest glacier in Iceland. At 3,300 square miles, Vatna (as the locals call it) was a landscape of unearthly beauty, and Bond was mesmerised by the view. An area of volcanic activity, the terrain was made up of undulating formations that were created by molten rock that was now, of course, frozen. Bond was well aware that the Lakagígar fissure, or Laki, Iceland's most destructive volcano, was situated in the area and that other active volcanoes occasionally erupted beneath the ice. This caused more damage there than it would if they were allowed to spout—pressure from the heat and steam actually lifted the ice cap, causing glacial melting and subsequent flooding.

Obstacles to enjoying glaciers were largely things of

the past thanks to four-wheel-drive technology and other modes of transportation. Bond knew that exploring glaciers was a unique experience. The Vanquish had been outfitted with special spiked snow tyres and a four-wheel-drive transmission so that he could drive right up to Gustav Graves's establishment, located not far from the town of Höfn in the southeast corner of the island. Graves had built a so-called ice palace at the edge of a frozen lake, complete with power plant, a hotel, and a laboratory.

Bond was extremely interested in learning more about Graves's activities. His initial instinctive distrust had developed into a belief that the man was a fraud. Unfortunately, there was nothing in Graves's recent activities that was in any way suspicious. The illegality of the diamonds might be hard to prove. Bond had spent the last several days digging up whatever he could find on Graves. He had no criminal record—but then again he hadn't much of a record at all. Very little was known about the man's life. No childhood friends, no former girlfriends, no other family members to talk to. This in particular aroused Bond's suspicions. How could someone become an international success overnight and be such an enigma? Bond knew that anyone with enough money could buy fame. This, though, was different. Graves had gained the trust of politicians, the admiration of the public, and had created a mystique that few entrepreneurs could equal.

Bond didn't like it. Graves hadn't paid his dues in life, and there had to be a reason.

The F985 led the Aston Martin some twenty miles out of Höfn to the broad glacier spur, Skálafellsjökull, after which the landscape presented a clean white slate.

Bond followed the directions that Miranda Frost had given him, drove for another half hour, and then ascended an icy, rocky ridge. He suddenly found himself looking out over the vast frozen lake. At the far end was a rock face where an enormous structure of interlinked geodesic domes was imbedded. Made up of dozens of octagon-shaped units, the domes resembled gigantic igloos with honeycomb-patterned exteriors. Next to the domes, wreathed in curling steam, was a futuristic geothermal power plant, laid out before an open-air hot spa. A security fence with a double gate surrounded the largest dome.

But what was truly impressive was the spectacular palace made entirely of ice. It sat on the frozen lake a hundred feet before the domes and appeared to be made up of several levels. It reminded Bond a little of the huge mansion covered in ice at the end of *Doctor Zhivago,* except that Graves's palace had a much more modern architectural feel.

As he grew closer, Bond could see that the palace was a hive of activity. Four-wheel-drives, snowploughs, helicopters, Ski-Doos, and television trucks were engaged in various tasks around the building. Some of the guests were playing golf on a temporary course fashioned on the lake.

Bond pulled up to the building and parked near a group of other sleek and expensive cars. Graves obviously had an elite guest list. Bond got out of the car and heard a jetlike roar that seemed to be coming closer. Like everyone else, he looked towards the source of the noise and saw a distant cloud of white shooting across the lake like a dust trail. Heat haze swirled in the wake of a fast-moving dot.

Bond moved away from the parking lot with his luggage and joined some of the other spectators. He could now see that it was some kind of bladed ice chariot, trailing rocket flames at what he guessed to be three hundred miles per hour. It was hurtling straight for the palace. Several men standing on an apron in front of the palace appeared to be waiting for the vehicle.

A parachute opened behind the ice jet, slowing it down. Then a grappling anchor paid out from the back, digging deep into the ice and pulling it to a stop near where Bond was standing. The men swarmed around the craft and one of them helped the driver out of the cockpit. Sure enough, it was Graves himself.

"Three hundred and twenty-four miles an hour," said the man, showing Graves a stopwatch. "A new personal best."

"Thruster two gave out, Vlad," Graves muttered, giving the man a sour look. Vlad looked as if he expected a reprimand, but then Graves saw Bond and gestured to another man to follow him. "Luggage, Mr. Kil."

The man called Kil, a huge brute of a man, lumbered forward and took Bond's bags.

"Well, there's a name to die for," Bond said. Kil ignored the quip.

Graves stepped up to Bond but again didn't offer his hand. "So glad you could make it, Mr. Bond. Been to Iceland before?"

"Once or twice. Never in this area."

"Here nature reigns supreme. What did you think of my run?"

"You looked like a man on the edge of losing control," Bond said as they turned to walk up the steps.

"Only by taking on the elemental forces can we affirm who we really are. Under the skin, I mean. Take your Donald Campbell. Nineteen sixty-seven. The *Bluebird*. Water speed record."

"Campbell died on his return run."

"But he died chasing a dream. Isn't that the best way to go?" Graves slapped Bond on the shoulder, then entered the palace. Bond was right behind him, but he hesitated when he caught the sight of a fuchsia-coloured Thunderbird pulling into the car park. The driver was none other than Jinx.

The foyer was surreal looking and disorienting, with light filtering through thick translucent walls. A huge tank filled with rare and exotic fish was built into one wall. Ice sculptures adorned white pedestals that were situated around the room. A gigantic chandelier hung from the ceiling and was covered in icicles. A long-haired snow-white cat with a sparkling diamond collar surveyed the arriving guests insolently from its vantage point on top of the reception desk. The world's media had gathered here and people were moving in all directions.

Bond was truly impressed. "Whereas you don't chase dreams, you live them . . ."

Graves seemed pleased. "You had better believe it, Mr. Bond. But it's true in another way. Perhaps you've heard that I don't sleep?"

"Yes, I have, as a matter of fact. How do you do it?"

"Years of conditioning. Sleep is a waste—there's plenty of time for that once you're dead. But yes, I do live my dreams. Wait until you see Icarus."

Graves strode off down a long curving umbilical passage that extended over the ice to connect with the domes perched on the shore of the lake. Bond looked over and saw Mr. Kil gesture with a nod of his head

that Bond should follow him in a different direction—
where Miranda Frost was waiting.

"Miss Frost," Bond said cordially.

"Mr. Bond," she replied with no warmth.

"A palace of ice? You must feel right at home."

"Hardly," she said, her eyes narrowing. "Gustav built
it just for tonight's demonstration. I'm told the human
element necessitates a precise balance of heat and cold."

"Built on a lake—I hope he's got the balance right."
Bond looked towards the passage where Graves had
disappeared. "What's through there?"

She led him further in the opposite direction. "The
diamond mine. And Gustav's living quarters. You
won't be seeing inside. He values his privacy even more
than his diamonds. Security is extra tight."

Bond was intrigued by her cool attitude. She stopped
in front of a door.

"This is you," she said. Kil slid back a huge slab of
ice to reveal a breathtaking suite, bedecked in fur.

Bond looked at Miranda and asked, "Would you like
to show me more?"

She gave him a disdainful look and walked away
with Kil.

Bond spent the next half hour in the suite getting
ready for the evening's presentation. He showered and
was amazed when the bathroom didn't melt. He turned
on the plasma television and watched as he dressed in
his tuxedo. It was a programme about Graves.

The man was standing in what appeared to be a giant
hothouse, home to all manner of rare exotic plants. Vast
palms arced over ferns, bromeliads, and weird succu-
lents. A waterfall roared behind him.

"My name is Gustav Graves and I'd like to welcome

121

you to Iceland—and my Biodomes," he said to the camera. "This is where my diamonds are mined, cut by the latest in laser technology. Deep below, my drills are carving away, stealing jewels from the dark. Then the lasers are let loose, cutting the stones and marking them with my Double G. And here, above, I convert the waste into fertiliser to grow new life that will in turn be processed into diamonds and coal."

Bond slipped on his dinner jacket and finished by straightening his tie. He flicked off the television and left the room.

The palace's ice bar was full of people dressed elegantly in tuxedos and evening gowns. Lighting cleverly used the ice to reflect a multitude of colours around the rooms. There was excitement in the air, and everyone seemed to be in a festive mood.

Bond stepped up to the bar and ordered, "Vodka martini. Plenty of ice, if you can spare it." The bartender acknowledged the joke with a wink and set to work. Bond took a moment to look around the room. He was searching for someone in particular, and he found her at the other end of the bar. Jinx was wearing a low-backed evening dress, and she looked as good as a Hollywood star.

Bond took his martini and walked over to her. "Mojito?" he asked, indicating the bartender.

She eyed him cautiously. "James. Here for the view again?"

"Magnificent as ever. But right now I'm only interested in endangered species."

"Does that include me?"

"Depends on what you're up to this time."

She knew what he meant and shrugged. "So I left you in an explosive situation. I figured you could take care of yourself."

"No wonder your relationships don't last."

"I'm just a girl who doesn't like to get tied down."

Bond wanted to get her in a quiet place and find out what she knew. She probably felt the same way. They both understood that they couldn't risk taking on the other. Covers could be blown.

Miranda Frost approached them. She was also dressed beautifully in a sparkling low-cut gown.

"Good evening, Mr. Bond," she said. "And Miss . . . ?"

Jinx cut in before Bond could introduce her. "Swift," she said. "*Space and Technology* magazine. Replacing Dr. Wiseman. We lost him to that new quasar in the Orion Nebula."

They shook hands, but Bond could see that Miranda wasn't entirely convinced by Jinx's story.

Miranda indicated Bond and said, "I take it Mr. Bond is explaining his big bang theory?"

"Miss Frost?" A member of the staff interrupted them. "The demonstration starts in five minutes."

"I'm on my way, Mr. Werner," she answered. She turned back to the couple and said, "Gustav's moment has arrived. Shall we?"

As Miranda walked away, Bond turned to Jinx and whispered, "Not Jinx anymore?"

"Oh, I'll always be a Jinx to you," she whispered back.

Bond looked to see where Miranda was going, moved a few steps, and turned back to take Jinx's arm—but she had vanished. He scanned the crowd around him but didn't see her anywhere.

13

Let There Be Light… and Love

The crowd moved outdoors to the large apron in front of the palace. The sun had set, but a bright full moon illuminated the area well enough for people to see. Vast video screens had also been set up, providing views of the proceedings for everyone. The TV cameras were shooting live and newscasters from around the world were already broadcasting their introductions.

Graves headed to a podium guarded by several security men. Bond noticed that they weren't so much guarding Graves as they were a large, open case that sat on a plinth next to the podium.

"Ladies and gentlemen," Miranda Frost announced. "A man who needs no introduction—Gustav Graves!" The audience applauded loudly as Graves stepped up to the podium and Miranda moved back. Graves waved, mouthed the words "thank you," and bowed. He then turned to the open case and manipulated an object inside it. Bond was unable to see exactly what it was except that it was some kind of curved metallic unit that filled the width of the case.

Suddenly the system came alive. An image of earth as seen from a satellite appeared on the video monitors. The crowd let out an awed gasp. Codes raced across the screens as Graves turned back to the microphone.

"As you know, I try, if I can, to give to the planet something in return for what it's given me—those little shards of heaven known as diamonds. Now, diamonds aren't just expensive stones. They're the stuff of dreams and the means to make dreams real."

Graves reached over to the object inside the case and worked a silver trackball. All eyes were on him, but Bond was busy scanning the area and the crowd. The domes behind the palace glinted in the light. What mysteries did they contain? His eyes moved from there into the audience and found Jinx. She, too, was not focused on Graves. Bond followed her gaze and saw that she was staring at three middle-aged Asian men wearing ill-fitting suits. They were watching Graves with animated interest. Investors, perhaps?

Graves continued to speak. "Imagine being able to bring light and warmth to the darkest parts of the world, grow crops year-round, bringing an end to hunger. Imagine a second sun. Shining like a diamond in the sky." He paused for effect and then commanded, "Let there be light!"

High above the earth, a satellite unfurled its silver sail and flowered to become an enormous mirror. The sun's rays hit it and reflected downward to the patch of white in the southeastern corner of Iceland.

On the ground by the palace, the shadows cast by the full moon began to mutate as a brightness grew on the other side of the sky. From the vantage point of the spectators, it appeared to be the formation of a new sun.

"I give you . . . Icarus!" Graves shouted.

The new sun cast a massive cloak of light. At first the crowd was too stunned to react. Then the applause began, and built until everyone was cheering—TV crews, the palace staff, the foreign dignitaries . . .

Graves shouted over the din, "At last the forgotten people can take control of their destiny!"

Bond now realised why Graves had chosen this setting for the grand unveiling. Beneath the midnight sunlight, the ice palace began to "sweat" gently. The outer skin was melting in the heat. Wisps of steam rose from the thick ice on the ground.

Graves ostentatiously donned a pair of sunglasses to face the icy glare, assuming the persona of a superstar miracle worker among his adoring and bewildered flock. The magic of it all had many people in tears.

Graves flicked a switch and the monitors changed to display a CGI animation of Icarus unfurling in orbit.

"Icarus is unusual," he said. "A mirror that thinks before it reflects. Its four-hundred-hundred-metre surface will inhale the sun's light and breathe it gently upon darkened cities."

Bond found Graves's face strangely unsettling in the artificial light. As he studied the man, Graves turned and seemed to be looking straight at him.

"It is for you," he said.

Suddenly the light went out and the moonlit shadows returned. The surprised and unnerved crowd emitted a collective gasp. This was followed by more applause.

126

Ever the showman, Graves grabbed the microphone and said, "Now *we* will brighten the night with our inner radiance."

Dance music started up. Palace staff opened the doors and began to usher the crowd back inside for the party. Bond hung back to watch Graves and his men pack up. The men called Vlad and Kil came to the podium, closed the large case, and took it away.

"Nice speech, boss," Kil said.

"You're a genius, Vlad," Graves said.

Bond stood in the shadows as Vlad and Kil headed around the outside of the palace and got into a Range Rover. They drove away from the crowd, back to the domes and the double security gates. Bond had an idea and headed for the Vanquish. It was time to see if Q's latest contribution to the free world was worth its weight in diamonds.

The guard patrolling the car park stopped and thought that *something* had changed, but he couldn't quite put his finger on it. He kept patrolling, blaming the sensation on being overtired. His shift would be done soon; he'd go and have a nice vodka and then fall into bed.

It would never occur to him that the Aston Martin had vanished.

The Range Rover pulled up in front of the security gates and Kil pressed a button on the dashboard. The gates opened and the truck lumbered through. No one heard the low purr and soft crunching of snow that followed the Range Rover inside before the gates shut. The truck pulled over and stopped. Vlad and Kil got out with the case and walked towards the big dome.

Bond stepped out of thin air, closed the door of the

invisible Aston Martin, and trailed the two men to the umbilical tunnel. Through the translucent ice, Bond could see them as he remained on the outside, tracking the pair as they walked towards the geothermal plant. They stopped at the connection to one of the domes. The shapes were blurry, but Bond ascertained that one of the men pressed his hand on a scanner to unlock the door to the dome. He figured that the scanner was of the biometric type, which read individual palm prints.

Once the men were inside the dome, Bond couldn't see them anymore. He moved further around the structure, past huge pipes that snaked out of the power plant. The sound of roaring steam attracted him to one particular pipe that passed through a valve marked HIGH PRESSURE RETURN VALVE—WARNING! DO NOT SHUT OFF WITHOUT CLOSING INLET VALVE!

Next to the pipe was a smaller ventilation pipe with a hinged flap on the end. Bond squatted and opened the flap to look inside. He got a view of a part of the interior and recognised the waterfall he had seen on the television in his suite. At the base of the waterfall was a pool set amongst a jungle of plants. A few fallen leaves covered the surface. This was obviously the "hothouse" where the diamonds were mined.

Bond looked down at the ground and found that he could see through the ice. Small dark shapes drifted past underneath him. He realised that these were leaves and that the pool actually fed into the lake. Bond filed this information away in his head and looked up. The shape of a figure was moving around on the other side of the translucent dome wall. From the size of the man, Bond knew it was Kil.

"Don't move," a voice behind him commanded.

Bond raised his hands, then turned abruptly and flattened the guard with a powerhouse to the face. He heard more of them coming, and they were between him and the Vanquish. There was no other way out. Unless . . .

Time to play, Bond thought. He quickly shut off the return valve and moved away. The sound of the steam increased dramatically as it built up and caused the pipe to explode suddenly, blowing a large hole in the security fence. Immediately alarms rang out as steam billowed out of the pipe and blanketed the area with a thick mist.

Bond hurried away from the chaos and stepped through the hole in the fence. He looked around for other guards, but the mist was so thick he couldn't see beyond four feet in front of him. He moved on as guard dogs began to bark nearby. Using his finely tuned sense of direction, Bond made his way to the front of the dome and moved along the umbilical tunnel until he came face-to-face with Miranda Frost. She held a gun with two hands, pointed right at him.

"Take your clothes off," she said.

Back at the dome, Kil and several guards had trouble holding back the two dogs. The identical black Dobermans had picked up a scent and were pulling their leads towards the palace. Kil shone a torch on the ground and saw tracks in the snow leading to the hot spa.

"This way," he said. They ran with the animals through the mist and came upon the steam-cloaked open-air hot spring. Bond and Miranda were in the water, naked, very close together and talking quietly between kisses.

"M warned me this would happen," Miranda whispered breathlessly.

"You're not as good at faking it as you think," Bond replied.

"Was I that obvious?"

"Tried a little *too* hard not to be interested in me."

"God, you're worse than your file says. I should have let them catch you. Now *I'm* exposed." She caught sight of Kil watching them through the steam and kissed Bond again.

"You're not fooling anyone. Put your back into it," Bond said. Miranda really turned it on then, making passionate moans and kissing Bond with fervour. Kil gave up, disgusted, and sent the other guards back with the dogs. The alarms soon stopped.

"I know all about you, Double-O Seven," Miranda murmured between kisses. "Sex for dinner, death for breakfast. Well, it won't work with me."

"That's better," he said, returning her enthusiasm.

Between kisses and whispers of sweet nothings, Miranda talked business.

"I so admire your restraint; you were here a full two hours before anything blew up. What were you doing at the mine?"

"Just letting off a little steam," Bond replied. "You were right about his security."

"Should have listened to me, you could have got yourself killed . . ." She bit him on the ear and wrapped her legs around his waist underwater.

"You're getting good at this," Bond noted.

"Hmm, so are you," she murmured. "Are we still being watched?"

"Oh, we fooled him. He left a while ago."

"And he couldn't even see what your hands were doing."

"It's all about attention to detail."

Then Bond noticed that a new figure was watching them through the steam—Gustav Graves. The man walked forward to the edge of the spa and said, "Excitement seems to follow you around, Mr. Bond."

Miranda gave a little shriek of embarrassment and ducked down in the water.

"Miranda, you give new meaning to 'public relations,' " Graves commented. "Don't let your devotion to work make you late tomorrow."

She smiled thinly at her boss, who then walked away.

Graves went straight to the hothouse and crossed around the pool, heading beneath the waterfall to where Vlad's workshop was located. Vlad was already there, making adjustments inside the Icarus control case. He looked up and smiled as Graves came in.

"Happy, boss?" he asked.

"Vlad, I've already told you once tonight that you're a genius," Graves replied. "Now show me the . . . modifications."

Vlad pressed a couple of buttons and the case smoothly yielded up the curved metallic object contained within it. It was a gauntlet, a brassard made of metal on which the trackball was mounted. Next to the gauntlet was a strange visor. The entire mechanism hummed.

Graves went to touch it, but Vlad stopped him. "The self-defence mechanism you asked me to build in . . . !"

"Fifty thousand volts?"

"A hundred," Vlad said proudly. He pressed a button on the arm and the humming stopped. Graves lifted the brassard excitedly. He held as if it were a priceless work of art.

"*Armed* and very dangerous," he said, entranced.

Bond opened the door to his suite and looked back at Mr. Kil at the end of the corridor. Bond smiled, and for once, Kil smiled back. Bond closed the door and went into the suite, which was now bedecked with lit candles. Miranda was waiting for him, anxiously sitting on the fur-lined bed.

"You'd better stay here tonight," Bond said. "Keep up the charade of being lovers."

"For one night only," she agreed. She started taking off her clothes. "But the way you're going, you'll get us both killed."

"Advance and the bullet might miss. Retreat and it never will." He removed his jacket, tie, and shirt. Miranda slid under the fur and admired his body. She noticed the scars and other marks on his torso.

"James, tell me," she asked. "What really happened in North Korea?"

"I was betrayed, that was all."

Bond slid his Walther under the pillow and got into the bed beside her. "Occupational hazard," he explained.

"You're different to what I expected," she said, studying his face. The cold blue eyes, the cruel mouth, the faint scar on his right cheek—they made him devilishly handsome.

"How so?"

"More . . . alive."

"So are you." He kissed her hard on the mouth, and she pulled back a little. She looked into his eyes, pulled him close, and kissed him back.

"This is crazy," she muttered. "You're a Double-O . . ."

"It's just a number."

He held her tightly against him and they began to make love.

14

In the Hothouse

It was the middle of the night.

The man wearing snow goggles and a balaclava padded down the corridor from the hothouse, went past Vlad's office, climbed the stairs to the second level, and approached the closed glass door that was the entrance to Gustav Graves's office. He slowly opened it and stepped inside the unusual room, which was made mostly of glass—the floor, the ceiling, the desk, and parts of the walls.

Graves was lying on a reclining chair. A curved screen—the same Dream Machine that had been used in the Beauty Parlour clinic in Cuba—covered his face. The device blinked with dancing colours as his eyes moved rapidly, scarily, beneath half-closed lids.

The stranger removed the balaclava and goggles and set them down on a desk. He moved to Graves and put a hand on his arm. Graves awoke, pushed the screen away, acknowledged his visitor, and stood. The two men regarded each other wordlessly and then began to converse in Korean.

"You look terrible," Zao said.

"You aren't looking too good yourself," Graves replied. The white-skinned Zao still looked bizarre and faintly reptilian.

Graves switched to English. "For just a little longer I must remain in this fiction."

Zao indicated the curved screen and asked, also in English, "You're still getting side effects?"

"For me, the insomnia is permanent," Graves answered. "But an hour a day on the Dream Machine keeps me sane. So . . . what happened to you?"

Zao narrowed his eyes and said, *"Bond."*

"He does get about, doesn't he?" Graves smiled and held his hand to his face. "But he knows nothing. I have been this close to him, and he had no idea who I really am." He paused, almost afraid to ask his next question. "Did you see my father after you were exchanged?"

Zao eyed Graves warily. "Yes. General Moon still mourns your death." Emotion suddenly overcame Zao and he bowed. "How strong you have been, to hide in the shell of the thing you hate!"

Graves, AKA Colonel Moon, put a hand on Zao's shoulder, then walked over to a mirror. He studied his reflection for a few moments, then his face convulsed in repulsion at what he saw. He smashed his fist into the mirror, hitting it again and again, splintering it into a thousand pieces in an attempt to destroy his despicable image. Zao watched him silently, allowing his

135

leader to release the tension that had obviously been building.

Finally, Graves calmed down and looked at the shards of mirror on the ground. They now made a fractured image of his face.

A warning buzz sounded on an electronic panel over the desk. A blue light flashed with the message: IN-TRUDER ALERT. Graves and Zao eyed each other and then Graves moved to the brassard on the desk. He pressed a button and it hummed with growing power.

Jinx was not only a world-class swimmer and diver, she was also adept at stealth. She could climb like a cat and retain her balance as skillfully as any tightrope artist. In fact, when she had been a little girl, she had wanted to run away and join the circus. She had made her father set up an elaborate structure in the family's backyard so that she could perform tightrope and trapeze stunts. She had been a star on her school's gymnastics team.

Jinx was superbly qualified to scale the geodesic dome silently and quickly. Wearing a black cat suit, she reached the top of the dome, easily cut out one of the octagon-shaped membranes, jammed a steel rod into the frame, and snaked her body through the opening. A wire attached to her belt fed out of the rod, allowing her to glide smoothly down to the floor of the hothouse. She detached the wire, pulled out a knife, and was ready to start hunting.

At first she was slightly intimidated by the size of the hothouse. Where to start? Looking around, she noticed the corridor leading behind the waterfall and figured that's where the offices would be. She slunk around the pool and made her way into the passageway.

A light at the end attracted her, as the door was slightly ajar. She went closer and saw that it was Graves's office.

She heard a strange humming noise coming from the room, so she slowly pushed the door open and entered. A man was lying on a reclining chair with one of the Cuban Dream Machines over his face. Graves.

Jinx drew the Browning from the holster at her side and aimed at the man's chest. She fired three rapid shots but the bullets went *thud* into a wall of bulletproof glass that she hadn't noticed. Cracks snaked across the barrier.

Damn! Why hadn't she seen the glass?

Before she could move, Zao flipped up the Dream Machine and smiled at her, his creepy face taking on even more of a reptilian appearance in the blue light. Startled, Jinx took a step back and was hit with a thousand volts as Graves stepped out from a hiding place and grabbed her with the weird gauntlet. She convulsed violently and fell to the floor, unconscious.

It was not quite dawn.

Bond dressed quietly in a black survival suit and covered it with his street clothes. He moved to the bed where Miranda was sleeping. He carefully lifted the pillow to retrieve his gun, but Miranda's hand covered it before he could touch it.

"James?" she whispered. "Be careful."

He took the Walther and said, "Go to your room. Lock yourself in. I'll come back for you."

Bond leaned over to kiss her softly on the forehead, then left the room.

The corridor was empty and quiet. He moved quickly

to the lobby and saw a guard behind the reception desk and another near the front doors. Looking around him, he saw that a few pieces of ice had broken off the lower edge of the corridor entrance. A food cart or something had probably struck it, Bond presumed. He reached down and picked up a piece of ice the size of a golf ball. He then got into position and threw it hard across the lobby, hitting the other corridor that led to the umbilical tunnel. Both guards looked up. The one at the door shrugged at the receptionist, walked over to the tunnel, and disappeared to check out the noise.

Bond slipped around the edge and into the lobby. He moved quickly out of the receptionist's line of sight and through the front door.

The early-morning air was cold. The sun was just beginning to rise, and it cast a magical golden glow over the frozen lake, which the wind had swept clear of snow. But Bond had no time to admire the view. He went to the car park and looked towards the security fence that surrounded the large dome. A sentry manned the hole that Bond had blown in it earlier. Bond removed the keyfob from his pocket and pressed some buttons. He waited a few moments until he heard the soft purr of the engine near him. He punched more buttons and the Aston Martin pixellated into view, having steered across the ice through the hole in the fence without being seen. Bond opened the trunk and then a strange flickering blue light, reflected off the interior of the hothouse dome, distracted him.

Jinx opened her eyes to a blur. The figure in front of her slowly came into focus and she thought she was having a nightmare. The face in front of her was white, with blue reptilian eyes. And then she recognized him. Zao, the terrorist.

She attempted to leap up but found that she was strapped tightly to a bench. Surrounding her were strange robotic devices with arms outfitted with lasers—state-of-the-art tools for cutting diamonds. The machines came to life when Zao pressed a button on a control panel.

"Why do you want to kill me?" he asked.

Then she saw that he was wearing the strange gauntlet on his arm. It was making the humming noise she had heard.

"I figured that was the humane thing to do," she answered.

Anger flashed in his eyes. Zao reached forward with the brassard and touched her. She jerked savagely as electricity surged throughout her body. She passed out again briefly, then slowly came to.

Jinx cleared her throat and said, "So you got a fancy cattle prod. Big deal."

"Who sent you?" Zao asked.

"Your mother. She's very disappointed with you."

He touched her again with the device. Jinx's body tensed and she gasped with pain.

"I'll let you in on a secret," Zao said. "This mine is a fake—but the lasers are real."

Another voice asked, "Why don't we use them?" Jinx turned her head and saw Kil standing off to the side. There was a sick gleam in his eye.

"We'll try this awhile longer," Zao replied. He reached forward and touched her again with the deadly brassard.

This time she screamed.

• • •

Bond squatted by the Vanquish so that he could operate in its shadow. Directing his new wristwatch at the ice, he switched on the built-in laser and began to cut a hole large enough for him to fit through. The process went very quickly. He burned away a small handhold and pulled the piece of ice off the ground, just like a manhole cover. Water flowed below, from the hothouse to the lake. He took a deep breath and slipped into the freezing-cold water. He then pulled the plug he had made back over his head.

Bond swam a dozen strokes, getting his bearings. He was in a cold, blue world that was completely different from anything he'd swum in before. Above him was an equally bizarre sight—the floor plan of the ice palace at its nearest point to the domes, practically a blueprint.

He concentrated on his heart, the exercise he had learned long ago in order to control his body. It was the only way to survive the intense cold. He swam harder, farther, until he knew that he was nearly there. A shaft of light shone in the distance.

Just as his breath nearly gave out, he surfaced in the hothouse pool.

Jinx was almost senseless. Zao had zapped her four times, each time sending her into temporary unconsciousness. He finally realised that it was hopeless.

"She won't talk." Zao offered Kil a gun. "Let's make it permanent."

Kil moved one of the diamond-cutting lasers into position. "Can I use the lasers?" he asked eagerly.

Zao turned towards the exit and said, "Don't leave a mess."

Kil considered the victim and made an artistic readjustment to the laser's position, then used a remote control to turn it on. The bright red beam shot out of the arm and cut into the bench between her legs. The bench began to inch slowly towards the beam. Kil grinned, then gagged the terrified Jinx.

Not far away, James Bond pushed his way through the hothouse foliage, the Walther in his hand. Someone was coming—he ducked behind a large bush and waited until a guard walked by. When it was safe to move, he crept slowly towards the waterfall. Another figure walked through, and Bond took cover again. When he saw who it was, he couldn't believe his eyes. It was Zao, wearing Graves's arm device.

Should I take him out now? he wondered. He had a clean shot. Bond raised the gun, but he waited too long. Zao disappeared through the foliage.

He moved on and came across the descender wire hanging from the roof. Somehow he knew who it belonged to. Bond kept going and entered the corridor behind the waterfall. A way down the hall a door was ajar, and through it he could see an arm strapped to a bench. He moved silently towards it and peered inside.

Bond was horrified to see Jinx gagged and strapped to the table. The laser was an inch away from her body. No one else was in the room. Bond rushed inside, grabbed the remote-control unit, and slipped the gun in his waistband. After a quick scan of the buttons, he pushed one and the moving bench reversed its direction. She was temporarily out of danger.

Bond reached up and freed one of her arms. She ripped off the gag herself and cried, "James!"

Too late—Kil leapt from nowhere and onto Bond's

back, knocking him forward. Both the Walther and the remote control went flying. When the remote hit the floor, the other three lasers came alive and began to shoot in a web of random fire around the room. Jinx tried in vain to free her other arm but couldn't reach the cuff.

Bond rolled before Kil could kick him in the stomach. The big man lost his balance and toppled to one side, nearly falling into one of the laser beams that were arcing back and forth across the floor. He caught himself just in time, but the distraction gave Bond the opportunity to get to his feet. Bond delivered a solid punch to Kil's face, but it hardly fazed the henchman. Kil deflected another blow with a powerful block that knocked Bond against Jinx's table.

"Stop dancing and do something!" she shouted.

The bench was still moving along its tracks, this time towards one of the other laser beams. This one would slice across her face in moments if Bond didn't act quickly. He couldn't see the remote but didn't have a second to look for it. He had to defend himself just as Kil came at him like a rhinoceros. The brute strength of the man slammed Bond against a control panel, causing a burst of sparks. Bond ignored the searing pain in his shoulder and brought his leg up high, kicking Kil in the chest. He fell backward just as the third laser suddenly changed its path of attack. It now swung back and forth, like a pendulum, between Bond and Kil. The beam traced a smoking, burning line in the floor.

This gave Bond the time he needed to find the remote. He saw it four feet away, lying within reach of both men. Kil eyed it at the same time. Both men knew that whoever got to the remote first could switch off the lasers, but then the other man would be free to attack with full force.

Bond launched himself at the remote and Kil hurled his huge body in the same direction. Bond got to it first and punched a button on the device, shutting off the swinging laser.

"Not that one!" Jinx cried. The laser she was referring to was now an inch from her cheek, burning a crevice into the table.

Kil grabbed Bond by the throat and squeezed. Bond attempted to push him off with one hand while grappling with the remote with the other. He finally succeeded in shutting off the beam that in another second would have destroyed Jinx's beautiful face. The robotic arms didn't stop moving around.

Kil picked Bond up by the neck and pushed him hard against the back of the door, slamming it shut. Jinx saw the desperate situation Bond was in and made a frantic attempt to reach the knife that was hidden in the small of her back. She was able to grab hold of the hilt and withdraw it. Taking careful aim, she hurled it at Kil.

The knife stuck in Kil's left arm. He turned to her, grimacing in pain, but he simply pulled the knife out. With one hand clutching Bond's throat, Kil twisted the knife in his other hand so that he could plunge it into Bond's chest.

Bond saw that one of the robotic laser arms was rearing up and pointing at the back of Kil's head. Kil raised his arm to stab his victim just as Bond pushed a button on the remote.

The laser drilled into the back of Kil's skull. His eyes widened and his mouth opened in a silent scream. Smoke drifted out of his mouth and he fell to the floor with a massive thud. Bond hit the remote again and shut off the laser.

"You killed Kil," Jinx said.

"A real hothead," Bond quipped. He gave her a leisurely smile and considered her situation.

"So, the girl who hates to be tied down . . ." He made no effort to release her.

"Get me off this thing!"

He was enjoying this. "You're CIA?"

"NSA. We're on the same side!" She struggled with the remaining cuff.

"Doesn't mean we're after the same thing."

"Sure we are," she spat. "World peace. Unconditional love. *And your friend with the expensive acne.*"

"Zao." Bond remembered and set about freeing her.

"I'd have nailed him back at the Beauty Parlour if you hadn't shown up," she said, getting off the table and rubbing her wrist. "Now he's back there with his weird psychedelic light mask. Must have brought it from the clinic."

Bond thought about this. "He couldn't have brought it. It was already here. It belongs to another Korean . . . his boss."

They went to the door but discovered that it was locked. Bond examined the biometric palm scanner beside it.

"I think Kil might have to give us a hand getting out of here." He went over to the corpse, grabbed him by the arms, and dragged him across the floor. The man was incredibly heavy. Bond heaved him upright against the wall and Jinx placed her boot on the dead man's chest to keep him there but it was no good. The weight of the corpse kept pulling him down.

"There is an easier way," Jinx commented. They exchanged a glance and Bond read her mind. He stepped back and positioned one of the robotic laser arms so that it was aiming at Kil's wrist.

"Shame he's dead," Jinx muttered.

Bond punched the remote and the laser zapped on.

A minute later the door slid open and Bond and Jinx crept out of the office. Bond looked out into the hothouse.

"Coast is clear."

They moved quickly to the closed door to the tunnel. Bond pressed Kil's severed hand against the security scanner one more time and opened the door. He then tossed the gory appendage into the foliage.

"I've got to get back," Jinx said.

"Go to Miranda first," Bond said. "She's MI6. Warn her to get out."

Jinx stepped through and looked back at him. "And where are you going?"

"Unfinished business." He closed the door between them.

15

Betrayed Again

Jinx moved through the crowded lobby, passing departing guests and continuing to Miranda Frost's room. She found it easily enough and knocked on the door, but there was no answer.

"Miss Frost?" she called out.

She tried the door and was surprised to find it unlocked. Jinx carefully went inside and called Miranda's name again. She went straight to the bedroom but found it empty, the bed not slept in.

Where was she?

Jinx heard a noise in the sitting room. She whirled around and took cover against the wall beside the bedroom door. She carefully peeked around the edge but didn't see anything in the other room. Perplexed, she moved out of the bedroom and went straight to the door of the suite.

She was locked in.

Gustav Graves walked into his glass office, flicked on the light, and found James Bond sitting at the desk. The Walther was aimed directly at him.

"So you lived to die another day, eh, Colonel?" Bond said.

Graves remained strangely calm. "At last," he said. "I was beginning to think you'd never guess."

Bond gestured for him to move away from the door. Graves complied.

"Was it painful?" Bond asked. "The gene therapy?"

"You couldn't possibly imagine," Graves replied, his memory stirred.

"Glad to hear it."

"There have been compensations, however. Watching you flail around in your ignorance. Granting you life, day by day, just to see if you'd get wise—when the answer was staring you right in the face. It's been such fun."

Through the doorway Bond could see Miranda approaching the office.

"Well, the fun is about to come to a dead end," Bond said as he stood.

"We only met briefly, but you left a lasting impression," Graves continued, ignoring the gun. "You see, when your intervention forced me to . . . present a new face to the world, I did my research—and chose to model the disgusting Gustav Graves on you. Just in the details—the arrogance, that unjustifiable swagger . . .

And your quips—a defence mechanism concealing such woeful inadequacy."

"My defence mechanism is right here," Bond quipped, indicating the Walther.

Miranda came into the room and, without a word, drew an identical P99 and pointed it at Graves.

Graves smiled and said, "So Miss Frost is not all she seems."

"Appearances can be deceptive," Bond said.

"By the way, did you ever find out who betrayed you in North Korea?" Graves asked.

"Only a matter of time."

"You never thought of looking inside your own organisation?"

Bond narrowed his eyes. He glanced over at Miranda and saw that she was now pointing her Walther at him.

"She was right under your nose," Graves said.

Bond kept his gun levelled at Graves and pulled the trigger. But instead of a bang, he heard only the hollow click of a bent firing pin.

"It was so good of you to bring your gun to bed with us," Miranda said.

Bond looked at her and repeated, with venom, "Occupational hazard."

Zao and several guards had been waiting just outside the door. They rushed in and relieved Bond of his weapon.

Graves was enjoying this. "I have a gift for sensing people's weaknesses, Mr. Bond. And Miranda's weakness is her strength—a most unhealthy appetite for winning. Ever since I arranged a lethal overdose for the true victor at Sydney, she's been my very own MI6 agent, using everything at her disposal—her brains, her talent, even her . . . sex."

"The coldest weapon of all," Bond said to Miranda.

Just as coolly, Miranda ordered, "Hand over the props."

Bond realised that he had no choice. He removed his wristwatch and handed it over.

"There'll be others after me," he said.

"Oh, you mean your American friend Jinx?" Graves asked. He looked at Miranda for an acknowledgement.

Miranda replied sardonically, "She's *chilling* in my room."

"Soon to be a victim of a tragedy. An ice palace can be such a dangerous place," Graves said, relishing the moment.

The world was caving in on Bond and there was only one thing to try. He looked at Zao and taunted him.

"You know, I've missed *your* sparkling personality."

"Very funny," Zao said. "But I've got a better punch line." He moved to Bond and hit him hard in the stomach. Bond doubled up and dropped to his knees. Zao punched him again, sending him to the glass floor. Bond could see the shrubbery of the hothouse below.

"Kill him," Graves said to Miranda.

Bond surreptitiously slipped Q's ring off his finger. Miranda moved to him and raised the gun, pointing it at his head.

"I enjoyed last night, James," she said. "But it really is death for breakfast."

Bond activated the ring and pressed it against the floor. The glass suddenly began to shake, as if an earthquake were gripping the world around them. The men in the room grabbed onto solid objects to steady themselves, but Miranda was thrown off balance. Then the floor shattered completely, causing Bond and Miranda to fall to the level below and disappear in the shrubbery.

Miranda was dazed but was able to stand after a moment. Her gun was lying a couple of feet away. She picked it up, looked around her, and thought she saw Bond running away through the foliage. She levelled the Walther at him and fired.

Up above, Graves rushed to the gallery, followed by Zao and the guards.

"Get him!" he cried. "But try to keep it quiet! The guests are leaving."

The men screwed silencers on their weapons as they ran down the stairs and disappeared into the jungle. Miranda joined the hunt as they fanned out. Every now and then one of them saw a flash of Bond running.

He's heading in the wrong direction, Miranda thought. They would have him cornered in a matter of minutes.

The *fwip* sound of a silenced pistol caught her attention. One of the guards was firing through the trees. She joined him and saw Bond running to the center of the hothouse.

"He's in the middle. Surround him!" she commanded.

The guards moved around the perimeter of the dome and began to close in. Zao joined the posse and gestured for the men to move in more quickly. The circle tightened, and Miranda was certain that Bond was trapped.

All of a sudden Bond shot up out of the greenery, flying a hundred and fifty feet up to the top of the dome on Jinx's descender wire. Zao and the others were caught by surprise, but they immediately raised their weapons and fired at him. Nevertheless, Bond made it to the cutout octagon and clambered through. They could see his silhouette through the translucent material and continued to fire.

Bullets zipped through the membrane all around him as Bond scrambled down the side of the dome. Keeping the descender wire attached to his belt, he threw himself down, a trail of bullets tracking his plunge. He touched down on the icy ground unharmed, detached the wire, and ran for the crowd of guests coming out of the palace.

He moved quickly to the car park where many guests were getting ready to leave. The Aston Martin was still there, safe and sound—but two guards were standing near it. Bond thought he could take them, but then he saw several more come out of the palace and head in his direction. Instead, he doubled back and headed for the first tee of the golf course. Perhaps he could take one of the Ski-Doos that were parked there.

As he approached the course, bullets ricocheted off the ice in front of him. The guards had spotted him and were set on cutting him off. Bond swirled around and ran in yet another direction, followed by a hail of gunfire. Then he saw the ice jet and bolted for it. Silenced bullets chipped into the ice as he leapt into the cockpit. He took a few seconds to study the controls, pushed a button, and hoped for the best.

The rockets blasted on and the vehicle shot forward.

Back at the palace, Graves witnessed Bond zooming off and turned to Zao, saying, "The pleasure of the kill is in the chase. Bring the generals in."

Vlad, standing behind Graves, pulled out his stopwatch and clicked it.

The ice jet soared onto the frozen lake and wobbled recklessly. Bond struggled for a moment with the controls, but he soon got the hang of it. It levelled out and accelerated up to two hundred miles per hour in no time. But in the rearview mirrors he saw that two of the Ski-Doos had been launched and were on his tail. They were fast little movers, but Bond was confident that the ice jet could outrun them. The only problem was that the henchmen on the ski-mobiles had automatic weapons and were firing at him.

Vlad watched through binoculars from the upper level of the hothouse as Graves ushered in the three Asian men who had been at the demonstration the night before.

"General Han. General Li. General Dong," he said. "I promised you a demonstration."

The man called Li said, "General Han here may have faith in you—but I have seen nothing to make me believe you are who you say. All you seem is . . . unwell."

Graves lost his temper and shouted in Korean, "I have created this facade for you! And now you doubt me! How dare you!"

The generals were shocked by this arrogant outburst. Graves moved to the case and removed the brassard. He donned it and put on the visor, then turned to a large screen beside him.

"Here, gentlemen," he said, "is your proof."

The screen came to life, displaying a satellite view of the Vatna Glacier. Graves manipulated the controls and the camera zoomed in closer . . . closer . . . until the screen was completely bright white. A black dot was moving against the whiteness, and the men realised that it was the ice jet, seen from Icarus. Graves punched more buttons on the gauntlet, opening the mirror sail on the satellite and directing its aim over the lake.

In the dragster cockpit, Bond felt a sudden wave of warmth. A bead of sweat trickled off his brow. He looked around him and noticed that the snow had grown brighter. Then he saw that the ice jet was casting a second shadow! He turned and looked at the sky.

There were two suns.

Around him, wisps of steam curled up from the ice. It was becoming incredibly bright and it was difficult to see. Then, without warning, a localised wind spiralled up, much like a small twister. The air was shearing, causing the vehicle to jolt about.

Graves and his spectators watched all of this on the screen. He kept manipulating the brassard, following the ice jet's every move.

"The Western spy runs . . . but he cannot hide. Icarus will lock onto the heat signature of his chariot," he announced.

The screen showed a huge circle of light focused on the area through which Bond was passing. The heat haze and evaporating snow seemed to warp the air around the ice jet, creating a surreal image that was disorienting.

Bond squinted against the painful light as the paint on the ice jet blistered in the heat. He changed direction, trying to avoid the intense beam, but it kept following him. He set his jaw, attempted to increase his speed, and turned again, but he just couldn't escape the deadly circle of light. Then, through the fierce glare, he saw something at his ten o'clock. Making a quick decision, he turned the ice jet towards the edge of the glacier. He knew it was madness—it was a sheer drop of six hundred feet to a lake filled with icebergs.

Graves watched the dot on the screen and understood what Bond was going to do. Just like an English gentleman, he thought. Better to die in a blaze of glory than boil to death at the hands of his enemy.

Vlad clicked the stopwatch and said, "He beat your time."

Graves snorted derisively. "So he's going out—at his peak."

Bond struggled with the controls, willing the ice jet to keep steady. The glacier's edge was racing towards him. Timing had to be absolutely perfect . . .

He fired out the anchor just as the dragster plunged off the edge and into thin air. The anchor skidded and scraped against the ice, desperately trying to latch onto something. The rope played out as the ice jet continued to fall. Bond shut off the engine and clung to the cockpit, waiting for the jolt he hoped would come.

The anchor finally caught the ice and embedded itself right at the edge of the drop. The rope jerked the ice jet hard, causing Bond to slam against the dashboard. Sudden darkness overcame him for a brief moment, and the next thing he knew was the sensation of eerie near silence. There was just the sound of the wind and the creaking rigging of the dragster as it twisted on the anchor line. He thought he must have passed out for a few seconds.

Bond looked down. Six hundred feet below, the icebergs were like teeth in an icy mouth that was waiting to swallow him. He looked up and saw that the glowing cliff edge was fifteen feet above him.

He carefully pulled himself out of the cockpit and

clung to the body of the ice jet. Slowly, painstakingly, he crawled inch by inch along the vehicle's exterior until he reached the anchor rope. Bond took several deep breaths and concentrated once again on his heart, forcing himself to stay calm and alert. He then took hold of the rope and began to climb up, towards the cliff edge.

Back at the palace, Graves studied the new development on the screen. The circle of light was straddling the glacier's edge. He could see skid marks in the ice leading to the glowing red heat trace of the hidden hot rocket motors concealed by the ice face. Graves smiled and drew his finger over the trackball. On the screen a red line graphic cut across the edge of the ice cliff.

"Time to draw the line," he said.

Bond felt the light intensify and move across the ice just behind the cliff edge. He heard a terrible cracking noise above him.

The cliff face was going to give!

Instinctively, he slid down the rope and landed on the suspended ice jet. A sharp report resounded like a cannon's boom and a huge crack snaked across the top of the glacier. As a hail of icy debris began to fall around him, Bond ripped open the parachute brake cover panel behind the driver's seat. There was another loud snap, and disintegrating lumps of ice and snow were suddenly bombarding him.

Then the entire top half of the ice face detached from the glacier and began to slide downwards—with Bond and the ice jet still clinging to it.

16

Fire and Ice

The huge ice slab crashed down into the water, throwing up a gigantic wave into which Bond and pieces of the vehicle disappeared.

Graves watched the screen with interest. There was now a new edge on the glacier, and the drop was nothing but a deadly white chaos of hundreds of tons of shattering ice. It would be impossible for anyone to survive it. He turned to the generals, shut down the brassard, and removed the visor.

"Global warming is a terrible thing," he said.

General Li bowed deeply and said in Korean, "Forgive me. *Colonel*."

The last of the ice face sank beneath the waves. A vast swell of water rolled away from the glacier wall, engulfing smaller icebergs.

Rising up over the brow of the wave and skimming over the rushing water, was a tiny figure borne aloft by the remains of the ice jet's brake-parachute. Bond had managed to fashion a kiteboard out of its hatch cover, and by sheer determination he was able to ride above the maelstrom. He concentrated hard on holding on to his improvised craft, for the forces of wind and wave were intent on knocking him to oblivion. Caught on the growing wave, with icebergs looming up towards him on all sides, Bond steered through the nightmarish obstacle course with great skill, half surfing, half flying over the accelerating water. If the stakes hadn't been so high, it would have been the most exhilarating ride of a lifetime.

Bond eventually approached an obstacle that was impossible to steer around. Up ahead was the sheer cliff of ice that formed the other end of the lake, and the huge wave was propelling him towards it at a tremendous speed. Desperate, he wrenched the ropes attached to the parachute and the board lifted out of the water. The makeshift kiteboard sailed into the air, leading the massive rush of water. The board dropped from his feet, but he clung to the chute and let it carry him over the cliff. He landed neatly on terra firma, just clearing the shower of water that broke over the bank. He dropped, rolled, and lay on the ice for a full three minutes before attempting to sit up. His felt his heart beating rapidly, nearly pounding a hole in his chest. His lungs gasped for breath and convulsed with pain as he sucked in the cold air.

After what seemed an eternity, Bond rose, removed the chute, and gazed towards the huge glacier at the other end of the lake and the fresh scar now in its face.

Nothing else mattered. Nothing was more important. One single thought turned over and over in his mind.

He was alive.

Miranda and Zao approached her suite with several gunmen flanking them. She nodded and Zao opened the door. The sitting room appeared to be empty. All was quiet. Miranda indicated to Zao to go on in. Eagle-eyed, he advanced.

As soon as he crossed the threshold, Jinx swung down from above and kicked him in the back. She landed like a cat, adopted a fighting posture, and then saw Miranda and the armed guards. Jinx straightened, aware that she was outnumbered. Zao recovered quickly and got to his feet.

"Nice moves," Miranda said. "Just like Bond. He was . . . so *vigorous* last night."

"He did *you*?" Jinx asked. "I didn't know he was that desperate."

Miranda gave her a brittle smile. "He won't be back. He died running, trying to save his own skin."

Zao relieved Jinx of her Browning and stepped back with Miranda. They went back into the corridor, leaving Jinx standing in the middle of the room. Zao punched the button to close the door and Miranda added, as an afterthought, "Your outfit is beautifully tailored. I hope it doesn't shrink when it gets wet."

The door sealed tight once again.

Zao and Miranda marched out of the palace and met Graves and Vlad in the front. The three Korean generals were in one of two Range Rovers that sat idling on the edge of the car park. Miranda and Vlad joined them and the vehicle drove away.

Graves spoke to Zao in Korean. "I leave the cleanup in your hands. When we meet next, it will be as victors. Keep your men out of the palace."

Zao said, "Our separation will not be as long as last time." The two men hugged, and then Graves boarded the second vehicle.

Bond trudged along in the snow with the parachute wrapped over his shoulders for warmth. It was hard going, especially after the ordeal he had just been through. He would have given anything for some form of transport and would even have been grateful for a cello case to ride on. His muscles were screaming and he felt dehydrated. Nevertheless he pushed on. Colonel Moon, AKA Gustav Graves, was clearly on the edge of madness.

The noise of an engine in the distance caught his attention. Bond scrambled up an icy incline and saw that a ski-mobile was heading his way. He considered the parachute around his body and got an idea. Bond ran back down and began to set his trap . . .

Moments later, as the machine passed a bank of ice, the parachute popped up from beneath the snow, pulled taut. The obstacle hit the driver in the face, knocking him off the vehicle. Bond appeared from behind the bank, leapt neatly onto the vehicle, and zoomed off toward the palace.

Then another loud noise, this time in the sky, alerted Bond to a new danger. A giant Antonov An-124 Condor heavy military transport aircraft swooped overhead. It descended for a landing somewhere in the distance, near his destination. He set his jaw and accelerated, pushing the Ski-Doo to its limit.

When he arrived on the outskirts of the palace property, Bond avoided being seen by driving behind an outcrop of icy rocks not too far from the building. He dismounted and watched from behind cover. It appeared that all the guests had gone, leaving just Graves's men. They were preparing to depart as well, working in the car park where the Aston Martin and Jinx's Thunderbird were stranded. An armed guard stood vigil over the cars.

Bond removed his keyfob, pressed some buttons, and watched. Spikes shot out of the Aston Martin's tyres and cover plates descended to mask the wheels. The Vanquish then shimmered and pixellated into a ghost of itself, completely disappearing from sight. The engine revved and the car crept away from behind the guard.

The man turned and was astonished to see that the vehicle was gone. Tracks in the snow indicated that the thing had indeed moved off the car park and around a bend. The confused guard decided to investigate. He followed the tracks around to where they seemed to stop and stood there, rubbing his chin.

Where was the damned car?

Suddenly a window opened before him in midair. Bond's fist shot out, grabbed the guard's collar, and pulled his face down hard on the top of the invisible car. The man slumped to the ground, unconscious, and Bond vanished as the window silently rose.

Bond studied the Vanquish's dashboard which was more like the control panel of an aircraft than an automobile. He brought up the heat imaging system and focused it on the ice palace. If Jinx was still in there, alive, she would show up on the monitor. But nothing was there. Everyone was gone. Had they taken her with them?

Wait. There was a small orange blob of life deep in the palace, in the area where the large suites were. It had to be her.

Zao had been spending the last several minutes patrolling the grounds and issuing orders to the remaining guards. When he came around the bend and saw the unconscious man lying in the snow, he raised his walkie-talkie and babbled into it. After a moment several gunmen on ski-mobiles appeared. As they awaited further orders, Zao looked around, scanning for the infiltrator. What he saw caused his jaw to drop.

One of the approaching ski-mobiles suddenly wobbled and warped as if he were seeing it through a distorting lens. Then there was a loud *clang* as the ski-mobile bounced backward off of *nothing* and the rider was catapulted through the air. He crashed down at the unsympathetic Zao's feet. Staring, Zao ran for a nearby Jaguar XKR.

Bond activated the communication system and punched in the frequency for London. He impatiently waited for an answer, not wanting to waste any precious minutes.

Come on! he willed.

Finally, Moneypenny answered. "James, where are you?" Her voice was filtered and sounded very far away.

"Skating on thin ice. Get M on the line. We've got an agent in trouble."

"Miss Frost?"

"Someone else. But Miss Frost is in *very* big trouble."

• • •

161

The Antonov landed on an ice field a few miles from the palace. Graves and his entourage were waiting for it in the Range Rovers. After the massive plane came to a halt, the ramp descended and the passengers prepared to board.

Graves opened the case and removed the brassard and visor.

"Time to give the American her bath," Miranda said. She grinned and followed the generals into the aircraft. Vlad stayed behind to assist his boss.

The gauntlet hummed and whirred as Graves manipulated the Icarus satellite into position. Once again, the sail unfolded and caught the sun's rays, this time directing them at the ice palace.

Leaving the satellite in place, Graves shut off the brassard and put it back in the case.

"Let's get aboard, Vlad," he said with a smile. "I'll handle takeoff."

Zao leapt inside the XKR and fired it up.

So the British spy has a few extras in his fancy Aston Martin? he thought. *Wait until he gets a taste of Moon's Jaguar . . . !*

Indeed, the XKR was a formidable machine with a 370-horsepower supercharged AJ-V8 engine that could match the Vanquish in acceleration from zero to sixty-two miles per hour in five seconds. The energy-absorbing front and rear crumple zones and wraparound bumpers gave it extra protection from those little mishaps that invariably occur when one is chasing enemy spies. Zao had no doubt that Moon's offensive and defensive additions to the car would give MI6's Q Branch a run for its money.

He brought up the thermal imaging system and the Aston Martin suddenly materialised ahead. Zao flicked a switch and a rocket fired from the Jaguar.

Bond, seeing the warning panel flash with the message TARGETED, threw the Vanquish into reverse and hit the accelerator. The rocket missed the car by a hairbreadth and exploded into an iceberg a few feet behind where it had been. Bond felt the concussion caused by the blast, but the solid armour of the vehicle protected him and it from harm.

Time to go and rescue Jinx.

The Aston Martin sped away towards the palace in a blur of tyre tracks and churning ice, but Zao wasn't about to let Bond get away so easily. At his command, machine guns protruded from the flanks of the car and began to fire. Bullets spewed and damaged patches of pixels on the Vanquish's skin.

Bond pressed a button and an armoured shield sprang up from the rear. Zao's bullets bounced off in an explosive roar. Bond hit another switch and fired back at the Jaguar with his rear fender guns. Apparently the Koreans had access to cobalt armour as well, for Bond's bullets ricocheted off the Jag.

Both cars thundered along, shifting gears and positions. Zao continued to shoot at the Vanquish, chipping off more pixels and uncloaking more and more of it. Bond finally turned off the cloaking mechanism and concentrated on avoiding the Jaguar. The goal was to get to the palace, but the Korean was cleverly making that task difficult with the Jag's weapons and by swerving in front of Bond whenever he could. Whenever Bond got a clear path to the palace, the Jag blocked him, pushing him further out into the ice fields. Eventually Zao pushed him towards a large glacier. It would take a dangerous manoeuvre to avoid hitting it, so Bond had to opt for the unorthodox. He fired a torpedo at the glacier and blew a tunnel through it. He hurtled through and came roaring out the other side. Unfortunately, Zao was right behind him. The Jag ploughed through the falling ice chunks, cleared the glacier, and decreased the distance between the two cars.

Zao's next ploy was to fire a heat-seeking rocket. The Vanquish's warning system alerted Bond just in time, and he managed to swerve out of the way. The rocket exploded against a snowbank, but the force was powerful enough to throw the Aston Martin over onto its roof with a crash. The car skidded along the ice as Bond hung by his seat belt upside down, helpless. Once the Vanquish came to a halt, Zao fired another heat-seeker at the target, which was now as vulnerable as a turtle on its back.

The warning system flashed again. Bond cursed aloud and then did the first thing that came to him—he hit the Passenger Eject button. In a fraction of a second the roof panel slid back and the seat slammed the ice, pivoting the car upwards and over—just in time for the rocket to whiz beneath it. The car then slapped down onto all four wheels.

Bond was back in business, if now lacking a passenger seat. He flattened the accelerator, turned the wheel hard, and smashed into the Jag, knocking it into a snowdrift. The Jag's wheels spun helplessly, sending up a tremendous spray of ice. Zao was trapped.

Bond prepared a torpedo, gripped the joystick, and placed his thumb on the trigger. Then he saw something bright out the corner of his eye, turned to look, and was horrified.

The Icarus beam was covering the ice palace. The structure appeared to be sinking into a moat of frozen slush, and its outer edges were beginning to crack. Flakes of snow swirled into the air, evaporating on the way.

Bond forgot about Zao, turned the car around, and gunned the engine.

17

That Sinking Feeling

Jinx had tried everything she could think of to escape from the locked suite. The icy windows were sealed tight; only a blowtorch could loosen the frozen frames. The door was a solid block of ice that a sledgehammer might smash to pieces, but unfortunately she was short one of those. If they hadn't taken her gun, she could have shot holes in the door, but even that probably wouldn't have done much good.

What had they meant about Bond? Was he really dead? Jinx didn't believe it. She didn't *want* to believe it. They seemed so sure, though. Jinx had done her research on Bond since the escapade in Cuba. She had learned a great deal about him and how dangerous he was. He was a formidable ally and had apparently come out of worse scrapes than this during his long career. Still . . . the Frost woman had seemed so confident. If

Bond's death was a foregone conclusion, then Jinx had to do a better job at finding a way out of that room.

The sound of a muffled explosion outside brought her to the window. All she could see was a billow of dark smoke coming from somewhere out of her line of sight. One of Graves's Jaguars was speeding along the ice, as if it was chasing something. Once it was out of view, she turned back to the room and challenged herself to find an escape route.

The heating and ventilation grille was built into the ice above the bed, but the opening was much too small for her to fit through. She moved the bed away from the wall, knocked over the desk, and explored every inch of the bathroom. There were no openings anywhere that could possibly be exploited.

What was she going to do?

Just then a bright light shone outside the window. She went back to look out but was blinded by the intensity of the beam. Jinx was gripped by terror as she realised what the light was from.

She backed away from the window and stood in the middle of the room, now desperate for some sort of salvation. As she scanned the room again, a drop of water fell on her forehead.

The ceiling was melting.

Then Jinx felt the floor lunge, as if something had impacted the building's foundation. Water began to seep out along the edges where the floor met the walls. She thought that either the ice palace was sinking or they were experiencing an earthquake. A series of loud pinging noises signalled that the ice was giving at the edges of the heavy structure. Terrified to the point of indecision, Jinx simply sat on the bed and stared at the icy room as the walls began to glow white and sweat. The drips increased in size and frequency until it seemed as if the place had massive leaks all over the ceiling.

James, if you're alive, you had better get here fast, was the last thought she had before starting to pray.

James Bond was driving directly for the ice palace when the entrance slumped and crashed down, sealing off any hope of getting inside. He had to swerve and skid across the wet ice to avoid crashing. With Zao still in pursuit, Bond turned the Aston Martin and drove around the palace structure to the umbilical tunnel, only to find that it, too, had collapsed. There was no way in or out.

Bond turned around again and sped through the car park. He felt the ground lurch violently as cracks snaked across the lake floor where it met the walls of the ice palace. With an awful groan, the entire building began to cave in on itself.

As Bond reversed directions again, Zao fired another rocket at the Aston Martin. It exploded just behind the car, but the force was powerful enough to lift the Vanquish into the air. The car crashed down in front of two Ski-Doos, clipped one, and hit the other hard—knocking it forward and causing it to smash into the sinking palace.

Bond couldn't believe the good fortune that the explosion had wrought. The ski-mobile had broken through a collapsing wall and created a hole large enough to drive through. He threw the car into gear and drove into the palace, lumbering over chunks of ice.

Zao also seized the opportunity and followed Bond in, with a Ski-Doo right behind him.

Bond found himself in the bar area. He shot around it, smashing into one of the balcony's supporting pillars. The Ski-Doo driver stopped, pulled out a rocket launcher, and prepared for the Aston Martin to come around the bar again. As he was about to fire, Bond's car clipped another pillar and most of the balcony collapsed. The driver jumped away to protect himself from the falling ice, but in so doing, he moved directly in front of the Vanquish, which smashed into him with a deadly *thump*.

Bond drove out of the bar and up the staircase, where water was cascading all around. Beams were falling left and right. Even with the spikes, the wheels slipped and slid, working hard to get a grip on the wet steps. The whole place was tilting at a crazy angle. Bond gunned the engine and the Vanquish miraculously gained some traction. It shot up the stairs, followed by the Jaguar.

The two cars zoomed around the curved corridor, one after the other. When he came to an intersection, Bond turned and skidded around the corner. The manoeuvre was successful in losing the Jaguar for the moment, so he took the time to look for Jinx again. He stopped the car at a balcony and engaged the radial thermal imaging system. There was a faint trace of body heat somewhere to his right and down a level. Bond saw that the corridor in question led to the area where Miranda's room had been. Jinx must be there.

Suddenly a livid heat image appeared on the system. The Jag was off to Bond's left. Bond was about to floor it when hunks of ice fell in front of the car, blocking his way out. There was a wall behind him, so he couldn't throw it into reverse. He looked at the Jag and saw that Zao had deployed what appeared to be a set of vicious bayonets out the front of the car. The Jag picked up speed and roared forward, intent on broadsiding the Vanquish off the balcony, skewering it at the same time.

Bond pressed another lifesaving button. The tyre spikes on the Aston Martin extended to twice their length. Bond revved the engine and slammed the car into reverse. The spiked tyres gripped the ice wall and the car climbed steadily upwards. The Jag was heading for the empty space with no time to brake. It flew off the balcony, ripped through the bar, and crashed into the water below. It sank through the blue towards darkness, surrounded by suspended tables, curtains, and chairs. Zao wrenched himself free of the seat belt and burst out of the car.

Bond drove the Vanquish down the stairs and stopped. He waited a moment . . . and finally saw Zao surface. Bond looked up to the giant ice chandelier teetering high above the pool. He quickly opened the secret compartment that held a backup pistol, removed it, and cocked it. He aimed carefully and fired a single shot, hitting the chandelier support. Like a gigantic stalactite, the massive ice structure plummeted directly on top of Zao. Bond watched the icy water slowly redden.

Meanwhile the ice shifted yet again and water gushed through the hole Bond had entered through, dragging the palace further down. Bond gunned the car and went down the rapidly filling corridor towards the executive suites. Finally, he saw her. Jinx was floating in what looked like an aquarium. The room had filled up nearly to the ceiling and fish were gliding around her.

Bond drove straight at the ice wall and crashed into it. Water poured out and Jinx was swept onto the hood of the car. Bond flicked the tiny switch on his ring and activated the sonic agitator, then pressed it against the windshield. The glass shattered, allowing him to pull Jinx inside the car. She flopped lifelessly into the seat. Dead?

Beams crashed all around, the palace tilted further.

It's not too late!

Bond floored the accelerator and headed for a wall. The Vanquish burst out of what remained of a top floor of the palace, which was now almost completely underwater. The car flew through the air and landed hard on the ice, then spun to a stop.

The palace disappeared under the surface of the churning lake.

Bond drove to the hot spa, stopped, and bolted out of the car with Jinx over his shoulder. He placed her down and swaddled her in bathrobes torn from a nearby hut. He pumped her chest and gave her the kiss of life. He peeled back an eyelid and noted that the pupil was fixed and dilated. Still no life.

No! Had his misreading of Miranda led to this? Was he responsible? Had he killed Jinx?

Bond was frantic to fight the hypothermia now. He rubbed her hands, her arms, her legs, her feet, wrapped her in fur . . .

"Come on!" he shouted. "The cold kept you alive. It must have kept you alive!"

He thumped her chest again.

"Come on!"

He listened and pumped again. He pressed his lips to her mouth again. He banged on her chest. Mouth-to-

171

mouth. Pump—Breath—Pump—Breath. As he tried to breathe life into Jinx for one last agonising time, realisation dawned on him. It was a lost cause.

Bond fell back and stared at her lifeless form. She was gone. All his efforts had been in vain.

Then there was a small choke. Her body jerked in a spasm. Water trickled from her mouth. She coughed again and more water surged out. Bond pulled her to him and cuddled her. He continued to rub her limbs, trying to restore circulation, his hands trembling. Jinx sucked in air and coughed again. Finally, she opened her eyes and looked around, disoriented. Bond stared at her and she noted his frenzied expression.

"Are you all right?" she asked.

He was so overjoyed that he started laughing.

At that moment, they both heard the roar of the Antonov taking to the skies. Bond looked up and saw the huge plane flying away with its evil passengers.

18

A New Moon

Gustav Graves sat alone in his quarters inside the huge Antonov aircraft as it flew halfway around the world towards North Korea. He felt extremely fatigued and needed a session with the Dream Machine to give him a burst of energy. The insomnia he experienced was more than just annoying; he knew that it was slowly driving him mad. Thankfully, the Dream Machine was something of a lifesaver; it kept him on track and focused. As long as he could spend at least an hour a day with the contraption, he was confident that his grip on reality would never falter.

After relaying instructions for no one to disturb him, Graves reclined in his seat and moved the curved screen over his face. At once, the machine hummed and the multicoloured lights began to flicker, mesmerizing him into a state of REM without the normal accompanying sleep.

He dreamed vividly, as he always did, about a variety of people and places. The face of his father swam in front of him, but Graves refused to feel any guilt over what was about to happen in Korea. The general was soon replaced by the image of James Bond, the enemy who had damaged his organisation and his plans. Bond was dead now and Graves could concentrate on the next step.

Graves's mind drifted, allowing the Dream Machine to take him into the depths of his subconscious. He began to remember events of the past year and how he had thrown away his life as Colonel Tan-Gun Moon to become a different person . . .

Colonel Moon had survived the plunge over the waterfall in North Korea by donning one of the lifejackets located inside the mothership and then covering his head with a bulletproof vest. The huge hovercraft fell for only a few seconds, yet Moon had the impression that it was suspended in the air for two or three hours. Whatever the time frame, the vehicle inevitably crashed into the water below the falls, and for a moment there was no light or sound. Moon clung to the vest and allowed it to absorb the impact that surely would have killed him otherwise.

After what seemed to be a lifetime of nothingness, Moon became aware of where he was. The water was cold, but not as frigid as he had expected it to be. It was unusually dark and he realised that he was underneath the hovercraft, which had capsized and was sinking to the bottom of the lake—taking him with it. Moon knew that he had to do something quickly or the life-jacket would be of no use to him.

Before he could think further, he felt the heavy vehicle blanket him, forcing him down on his back on the muddy lake floor. Because of the shape of the craft, though, it didn't crush him. His body was entombed in the space between the bottom of the lake and the hovercraft deck, which was now like a cover above him.

Moon almost panicked but got ahold of himself as soon as he remembered where he was and what he had at his disposal. Most of the weapons and military equipment had been secured to the hovercraft deck and were still there within arm's reach. Best of all, the Tank Buster was lying miraculously in the mud next to his legs.

The colonel picked up the large gun and twisted his body so that he could aim it at the side of the hovercraft deck. He was careful not to fire it at any of the assorted missiles and other explosives that were within a few feet of him. A nice blank spot on the hovercraft side would do nicely . . .

Moon squeezed the trigger and felt the violent recoil even in the depths of the lake. The muffled boom was loud and it shook the ground he lay on. A thick cloud of mud, sand, and bubbles swarmed around him, completely obscuring any visual confirmation of his success.

His lungs were bursting now—he had to move. Blindly, he crawled like a sand crab towards the hole he hoped was in the side of the hovercraft. Feeling his way through, he found the jagged edges of the cavity and thrust his body through it.

He was free.

175

Moon surfaced and gasped for breath. He lay there for a few minutes, allowing the momentum from the falls to push his body along, away from the cliff edge. He looked up towards the temple, where he had left the British spy. It was too far away to see any activity. Surely Bond would assume that he was dead.

Given the current situation, that was exactly what Moon wanted him to think.

Colonel Moon had many places in which to hide. He had installed safe havens all over North Korea that even his closest advisors knew nothing about. Now Zao was the only man who was aware that Moon had survived the hovercraft ordeal. They met at a prearranged rendezvous near P'yŏngyang and drew up the plans that would set in motion the events that occurred while Bond sat in a North Korean prison—and it was time to call Miranda Frost again.

The Dream Machine took Graves back to that time and place as he remembered the chain of circumstances.

Moon and Miranda had met when they were on the fencing team at Harvard and they developed a mutual respect for each other that they maintained after graduation. Moon was a young, vigorous, and handsome Asian man with wealth and power. Miranda Frost was attracted to him, but not necessarily in a sexual way. Likewise, Moon wasn't drawn to the Western woman in a physical sense. In fact, he was not much of a sexual being. He had had his share of women, but he had put aside carnal desires to concentrate on other things. His sole aim was to run North Korea and defeat the South, bringing the West to its knees.

When she had first met Moon, Miranda was a woman

who was loyal only to herself. She was intelligent, athletic, and beautiful, but she cared not a whit about her country or fellowman. Moon could see that she was someone who looked at the world as a place filled with adversaries to be overcome. Miranda had told him that she was an only child. Her mother had died during childbirth and her father had essentially forced her into the roles of both daughter and wife as soon as she was old enough to work around the house.

"When I was fourteen, I killed my father," she told Moon. "Well, that's not entirely true. But I caused his death."

"How so?" Moon had asked her.

"He was allergic to bee stings. He always bragged about surviving a nearly lethal sting when he was a teenager. We lived in Kent in a rural area. I used to go for long walks to get out of the house. One day I discovered a beehive not far from our property. I went back home and found a jar. I poked some holes in the lid with an ice pick and then I went back to the beehive. I wasn't afraid of the bees. I had been stung once when I was younger and I knew that I wasn't allergic to them."

"What did you do?"

"I trapped three of them in the jar and brought them back to the house. After my father returned from work that evening, I went outside with the jar and opened the car door. I let the bees loose inside and shut the door."

"What happened?"

Moon distinctly remembered the wicked smile that had spread across Miranda's face. "By the time my father went to work the next morning, the bees were angry and hungry. He got into the car, started it up, and drove out onto the main road. The bees attacked him and the car smashed into a lorry. He survived the crash, barely, but the bee stings caused his throat to swell so badly that he was asphyxiated. He was dead before the ambulance arrived."

Moon admired her ruthlessness, and they became allies against the world.

A few years after they had both left Harvard, Colonel Moon met Miranda again in Sydney, at the Olympic Games. She was on the British fencing team and was expected to come in second place. A Russian athlete had the edge, but Miranda was determined to beat her. Moon was there as an observer, since North Korea didn't participate in the games. He admired Miranda's ability and thought she should win. It was time to involve her in his plans.

It wasn't difficult. Colonel Moon and Miranda developed an unholy alliance in Sydney based on a mutual interest in power. Moon liked to rule and Miranda liked to win.

"I can guarantee that you will receive the gold medal," Moon told her.

"Really? How?" He had her attention.

"That's my secret."

"What do I have to do, sleep with you?"

"No, nothing so crude," he said, reaching out and stroking her golden hair. "My price for this service would be your undying loyalty."

"You already have that."

"Even though I'm a military radical in a Communist country?"

"Oddly enough, I find that appealing," she answered.

Colonel Moon poisoned the Russian fencing champion the night before the big match. When the moment of truth finally arrived, she managed to defeat Miranda on the floor, as everyone had predicted. But an hour after the bout, the Russian dropped dead, and the ensuing autopsy revealed that she had overdosed on steroids. She had suffered a heart attack. Miranda was declared the winner—she got her gold after all.

Miranda went back to England and Moon returned to North Korea. They kept in touch and Moon paid her to supply him with information. She pursued a job in the Secret Service so that she could help her mentor and friend, the only man she thought she could trust.

Graves's dreams shifted forward in time to his decision to alter his appearance and his identity. He had called upon Miranda to help him. After all, it was she who had set up the diamond connection in Africa and it was she who had identified Bond as the diamond merchant's impersonator.

"Have you ever heard of the Beauty Parlour?" Miranda asked.

"No. What is that?"

"A place in Cuba where people go who want to change their lives."

"How do you know about this?"

"Through my work with MI6."

She told him how she had learned of Dr. Alvarez and his Cuban clinic, where international spies and criminals could, for a price, change their identities. MI6 only knew this as a rumour. Miranda had kept her research to herself. The DNA replacement therapy was dangerous and experimental, but it worked. After some inves-

179

tigating on his own, Colonel Moon agreed to undergo the procedure.

Moon travelled out of Korea via discreet channels, paying for everything with his immense wealth. He took an indirect route, through Africa to South America and then to Cuba. He was at the clinic for a month, submitting to the terrible pain that accompanied the transformation. When he emerged from the Beauty Parlour, he was Gustav Graves.

Next came the difficult task of creating a life for his new persona. Graves went back to Africa and used his old connections to study diamond mining and processing. While he was there he used his influence to bribe officials and create false records indicating that Gustav Graves was an orphan from Argentina. He let it be known that he'd learned the diamond-mining craft as a child labourer. Most details were conveniently left out of the records so that he would always be a mystery to the public, but there was enough to make him seem legitimate.

Graves then enlisted the services of another colleague he had met in Africa. Jan Ericsson was a hard-drinking Icelander with a long, disreputable past who had made a fortune mining illegal diamonds in Africa and often sold his services to various warring factions. Back home in Iceland, he had opened a modest mine located underneath the Vatna ice cap and later announced a small-scale discovery of diamonds within it. He used the mine as a cover to distribute the African gems. The mine was, of course, a barren one—it contained no diamonds and never could—but Ericsson had conceived a perfect way of concealing the illegal origins of irresistible gems. So the conflict diamonds that Colonel Moon had used to finance his operations in North Korea had come from Africa via Iceland.

Graves and Ericsson did a great deal of business together and Graves flattered and beguiled Ericsson into closer friendship. He regarded the Icelander as a gross, blundering fool who had stumbled upon an idea that could be a passport to immense wealth, greater than Ericsson could ever dream of. One night when Ericsson was very drunk, Graves talked him into making him a partner in the enterprise.

"My friend," Ericsson said, slurring his words, "I am happy to do this. After all, my doctor tells me that my health is bad. I may not live long. I have no family. You are my best friend."

Graves humoured the man, pouring him another drink. "And I feel the same way about you, Jan. You're like a father to me."

Tears came to Ericsson's eyes. "Then let's sign the papers and be done with it. That way, if something ever happens to me, all this land will be yours."

Ericsson produced the documents, and they both signed them and shook hands. Ericsson gave Graves a huge bear hug and then fell back into his chair with a satisfied belch. Within a few minutes, he was snoring loudly.

Graves stepped over to his desk, opened a drawer, and removed a .357 Magnum pistol. He pointed it at Ericsson and calmly shot him in the head. Without a twinge of conscience, Graves then proceeded to execute three more men who were closely associated with Ericsson. Later that night, he buried the four corpses deep beneath the ice in the diamond mine.

Then Graves went public, announcing his discovery

181

of a magnificent new lode in the obscure Vatna diamond mine and producing the documents that proved that the land was all his.

Once he was established as a legitimate diamond producer, he could trade openly and profitably in the world's diamond centres: Antwerp, Tel Aviv, and New York. He could source conflict diamonds at very little cost to himself from the desperate, war-torn countries of western and southern Africa at an enormous personal profit. This combined with high-profile trading of famous legitimate diamonds made him the most powerful figure in this lucrative and dangerous trade.

Graves removed the Dream Machine from his face and stretched. The remnants of the dream stayed with him, though, and he continued to reminisce as he looked out the window at the sea of clouds in the sky.

It had taken only months for Graves to amass a fortune, build an empire, create a corporation, and begin to make headlines. He had surrounded himself with people of his choosing who would be loyal at all costs. Vlad, the Russian, was an aeronautics engineer who had a special gift for designing satellites. Kil, an Icelander, was particularly adept at enforcing Graves's orders. Miranda Frost managed to attach herself to Graves by persuading MI6 that she was working undercover. Graves's unimpeded progress was briefly interrupted by Zao's arrest in China, so Miranda brokered the deal to exchange Bond for Zao, managing to cast suspicion on Bond in the process.

The plan had worked beautifully, and fell into place even faster than any of them thought was possible. A week before Bond's release, the Icarus satellite was launched into space. Gustav Graves enjoyed the support of Iceland and the United Kingdom as well as that of the media and the jet set to which he catered and moved within. He had accomplished the impossible. Colonel Moon had become a completely different person, created a favourable public image, built a weapon of mass destruction under the very noses of his opponents, and totally fooled the world.

He had pulled off the most audacious infiltration into enemy territory since the days of the Trojan horse.

19

Korean Standoff

A week passed before Bond was back in South Korea at the edge of the Demilitarized Zone. After extensive debriefing with both MI6 and the NSA, he and Jinx had finally convinced their superiors that Gustav Graves was in fact Colonel Moon and that he was up to something of international concern. Details of the Icarus satellite were examined, and there was much debate as to whether it should simply be destroyed.

In the meantime, it was apparent that North Korea was amassing a large military force on its side of the 38th Parallel. South Korea responded in kind with their own buildup of defences. M and Robinson had flown once again to the area to oversee the situation and were working with the United States advisors to the South Koreans.

Jinx flew into Seoul from Los Angeles and met Bond

at the U.S. Army base where he had spent the few days recuperating from his prison ordeal. He had not enjoyed being reminded of those dark times, but he did his best to bury the memories. The days since the events in Iceland had been spent with various high-level British, U.S., and South Korean military personnel in an effort to outline a sensible strategy against Graves. Bond had also used the time in the base gym and shooting range to work out sore muscles, strengthen his body, and hone his firearms skills. As for Jinx, she looked well and rested after her week's leave in America. Bond thought that she looked beautiful, even in army fatigues.

"Hello, handsome," she said, giving him a big kiss. "I've missed you."

"Likewise," he replied. "Come on, they're waiting." He led her to an army Jeep and threw his duffel bag in the back. The driver couldn't believe his good fortune when Jinx stepped in front beside him.

"How did you get on with your people?" she asked.

"You mean convincing them that Icarus was a viable threat?"

"Yeah."

"M is taking it seriously. I'm not sure about the military."

"My boss, Falco, refuses to acknowledge my report. He's probably waiting for a demonstration," she said.

"Let's hope he doesn't get one."

The Jeep drove north to the command centre just south of the Demilitarized Zone. They entered the United States–controlled bunker and passed two watchtowers, more Jeeps, helicopters, manned antiaircraft positions, and dozens of soldiers. The driver took them into a vast hangar filled with more helicopters and military vehicles. The place was buzzing with activity as Special Forces soldiers geared up for action. Finally, the Jeep stopped inside a covered bay. A signal was given and the platform lowered into the bunker, where Charles Robinson was waiting to greet them.

"James," he said. "Jinx."

"Mr. Robinson. Bring us up to speed, please," Bond said.

They headed down a corridor as Robinson spoke. "Another division's just mobilised north of the DMZ. Eighty thousand troops and counting."

"And another million in reserve," Jinx commented.

"Moon's father won't let this turn into a war," Bond said.

"General Moon is under arrest," Robinson said. Bond stopped walking. "The hard-liners staged a coup last night. They've got him under lock and key."

Bond's face turned grim and then he continued moving.

They went into the bustling operations room, where South Korean and American intelligence and military analysts were busy studying satellite images and a large illuminated map of the 38th Parallel. A two-star U.S. general seemed to be dominating the centre ground with his Korean opposite number. Keeping back in the shadows was NSA chief Falco, who was standing with M. They appeared to be in the middle of a tense discussion.

M was attempting to keep her voice down, but it still carried across the room. "The fact remains that you deliberately misled me by implicating Bond. If you'd told us about your agent at the Cuban clinic—"

"She'd be dead by now," Falco countered. "Your mole would have made sure of that."

"We wouldn't have had a mole at all if you'd disclosed the fact that Miss Frost and Moon were on the Harvard fencing team together."

She turned and saw Bond and Jinx. Her last words were perhaps meant for Bond's ears as much as for Falco's. "Knowing whom to trust is everything in this business," she said.

Falco followed M's gaze and turned to Bond and Jinx.

"Ah, James Bond," he said. "Just in time for the fireworks."

Jinx shrugged and said to Bond, "Everyone has a boss. This is mine."

Bond fixed Falco with a hard gaze. This was the man who'd had M lock him up and then had falsely identified him as the destroyer of the Beauty Palour. Falco dropped the smile, realising it wasn't working.

"Don't believe everything she told you about me," Falco said, unnerved. "I'm not *all* bad."

Bond wanted to hit the man, but instead he said, "Let's get down to business."

Falco nodded and cleared his throat. "We're at DefCon Two, but the good General Chandler over there isn't worried. Just another manoeuvre to see if we blink. And if the North does go south—it goes south big time. You don't just stroll through the world's biggest minefield."

"No," Bond said. "You need some kind of edge. Icarus."

"Oh, yeah, your giant space mirror," Falco said dryly. "We're taking care of that. ASAT launch in one hour." He looked at Jinx and rolled his eyes. "Though I hate to waste a good missile."

Jinx flared a little. "Icarus isn't like our lame-assed covert weapons. It actually *works*."

"I've seen your report," Falco commented.

"I've seen what it can do," she countered evenly.

Bond ignored this exchange and moved to look at the screens.

"There's only one way of being sure," he said. "Where's Graves?"

M pointed out a screen featuring a satellite view of an air base. Bond recognised the distinctive shape of the Antonov.

"In the middle of a North Korean air base," she said.

"Right where we can't touch him," Falco added.

"You can't," Bond said. "But I can."

He turned to M and looked into her eyes. All that had happened between them had been just a prelude to this moment. After she had doubted him, after she had used him once he'd proved that he hadn't cracked . . . would she now show some faith?

Falco broke the silence. "We're here in case things escalate, not to make sure they do. No incursions into the North. The president gave me a direct order."

"So when did that ever stop you?" Jinx muttered.

M hadn't taken her eyes from Bond's. Finally she said, "You make your own decision, Mr. Falco. But I'm sending in Double-O Seven."

Falco winced and said, "You think I'd leave this in the hand's of the Brits?" He looked at Jinx and ordered, "You're going with him," as she spoke up simultaneously and said, "I'm going with him." Falco controlled his desire to reprimand her for her forwardness, then nodded curtly.

• • •

The United States Air Force Chinook helicopter flew over the Demilitarized Zone after loading its special cargo. Bond and Jinx put on camouflage gear and armed themselves with pistols, combat knives, and grenades. Bond was additionally equipped with an L42A1 sniper's rifle. After checking coordinates and radioing the operations room that they were ready, the couple went into the back of the helicopter where the cargo was.

The ramp lowered and two Switchblade jet gliders rolled out backwards, Bond and Jinx riding them like low motorcycles. The two sleek black craft dropped a few feet before jet engines kicked in, thrusting them both forward.

They flew quietly and at low altitude. As the Switchblades were made of stealth material, there was little chance of being seen by radar, but because it was still daylight, there was always the possibility of a visual sighting.

Below them was the surreal landscape of the wartorn no-man's-land that Bond remembered from his earlier experience in Korea. The bombed-out terrain, with its tank traps and derelict vehicles, looked like the remains of a long-lost civilisation, the victim of its own mindless self-destructiveness. Down there was where the dreams and lives of countless men and women had ended, creating a land of sorrow, despair, and ghosts.

Before long they jettisoned the Switchblades and parachuted into a dense wooded area just as the sun was dipping below the horizon. Jinx's chute caught on the branches of a tree and she was jerked hard by her harness, but then the branch broke and she landed on the ground.

189

"I'm okay," she said before Bond could ask.

They removed the parachutes, bundled them up, and hid them in some bushes. Without another word, they started moving through the woods towards their target.

Back in the operations room, Robinson received confirmation from the Chinook and reported, "They've entered North Korean airspace."

Falco noted that the young man's hand was shaking slightly as he wrote down the time of the message. "Relax," the NSA advisor said. "If *our* radar can't see those Switchblades, the North Koreans sure as hell can't."

Robinson nodded and concentrated on the exchanges on the radio.

Falco turned to a large screen that displayed the position of the ASAT missile, closing in on the Icarus satellite. He looked back at M, who stood with her arms folded.

"Hope you're not superstitious," Falco said. "This is one big mirror we're about to break."

M ignored the comment. She was restless and unable to sit still. She had sent Bond into dicey situations before, but surely this was one of the most dangerous. She didn't want to see him stuck in another military prison, or worse.

Still . . . she knew that he was aware of the risks.

The North Korean bunker where Gustav Graves was studying battle plans with Generals Han, Li, and Dong was a stark contrast to its U.S. equivalent. It was decidedly low-tech, with very little sophisticated equipment. The hard-liners now in charge of the military were united in purpose. Colonel Moon knew that the will to win was more powerful than expensive materials that rarely functioned properly.

Vlad approached his boss, who was now dressed in a North Korean uniform. "They've launched against Icarus," he warned.

Moon/Graves considered this but was unfazed. "Leave it on automatic," he said.

High above the earth, Icarus picked up the ASAT's signal and suddenly rearticulated and focused its reflectors on the threat climbing out of the atmosphere. The manoeuvre took twelve seconds. The sun's rays, invisible to the naked eye in space, hit the mirror and bounced towards the missile with power and heat. The missile began to shear and shake, its skin glowing with intense heat. The vibration increased until the missile ultimately tore apart in a massive explosion. Icarus then returned to its former articulation, unharmed.

Vlad noted the flashing lights in the open control case and proudly announced, "Threat eliminated."

Graves nodded casually, but the generals were clearly impressed.

In the operations room south of the 38th Parallel, Falco and General Chandler watched the event on the screens, which now depicted Icarus alone in the sky.

"Now, why don't we have one of those?" Falco asked wryly.

The general picked up a phone and gave an order. "Mobilise the South Korean troops."

A few feet away, M looked at Robinson and asked, "Still no news on Bond?"

Robinson shook his head and pursed his lips.

• • •

Bond and Jinx cut through the perimeter fence surrounding the North Korean air base. Communicating through tiny headsets, they moved stealthily in the dark, sticking to the shadows. The Antonov stood on the asphalt some hundred metres away. Its loading ramp was down and was the centre of activity. Dozens of troops occupied the area and many high-ranking soldiers were in the process of boarding the plane.

"What now?" Jinx asked through the headset. "There are a lot of men."

"See the shadow of the hangar?" Bond gestured to a long shadow cast by a tower floodlight. Between the edge of the shadow and the plane was a wide-open space of about thirty feet. "If we can get over there, the shadow should give us plenty of cover. The trick will be to move to the plane without being seen. Underneath it's dark."

"We'll be exposed for a few seconds."

"We have to take the chance. Come on."

They ran along the fence and then moved to the hangar. Staying in the shadow, they waited until most of the troops had turned away to gather more cargo.

"Now!"

Bond and Jinx bolted into the brightly lit open space and made it to the nosewheel in three seconds. They remained still until it was certain that they hadn't been seen. The timing had been fortuitous; seconds later a Ferrari roared out of the hangar and approached the Antonov, escorted by three Jeeps. Bond swung the L42A1 off his shoulder and aimed it. Now was as good a time as any to take out the prime target.

"Do you have a clean shot?" Jinx asked.

He didn't. The Jeeps blocked the sports car, but Bond

got a glimpse of Graves as he drove straight onto the ramp and into the hold. Then the ramp started to rise.

"Damn," Bond muttered. "We'll be seen." He slung the rifle back on his shoulder and moved to one of the rear wheels. "Come on."

He leapt onto the downstrut of the wheel just as the plane began to taxi. He held out a hand to Jinx, who was running alongside.

"You've got to be kidding," she said.

"I've done it before. Easier than it looks."

He pulled her up onto the wheel strut as the plane accelerated down the runway. They clung to each other and to the strut as the wind pummelled them, threatening to rip them away. The plane lifted off and began to climb into the night sky, but the two stowaways held on as the wheels were pulled in.

Jinx followed Bond through a hatch and into the darkened hold, where a Mil Mi-34 Hermit helicopter sat in front of the Ferrari and a Lamborghini. After making sure there were no guards in the hold, they climbed a ladder that took them to the Antonov's living quarters. They moved quietly down a passageway, turned a corner, and stopped. Someone was coming. Jinx pulled Bond through a door just as Miranda Frost walked by in the company of a few guards. Jinx peered around the door and saw her enter a room at the end of the corridor.

In the plane's cockpit, Gustav Graves gave final instructions to the pilot and then descended a ladder to a specially built observation bay. Located in the Antonov's nose, the room was dominated by a conical window. At the rear, the roof rose towards a giant angled semitransparent glass screen that depicted the entire Korean peninsula and Japan. Several monitors and instrument banks occupied the walls, and the gauntlet that controlled Icarus sat on a pedestal in the centre. Vlad stood over it, making some minor adjustments as the three generals stood behind him.

"Excellent takeoff, if I may say so," Vlad said to Graves.

"Don't grovel. You'll never take Kil's place."

Graves paid no attention to Vlad's wounded expression and went over to study the screen.

Back in the living quarters, Bond and Jinx continued their reconnaissance through the corridors and came upon the stateroom they were hoping to find. The sound of a guard approaching forced them into the shadows, where they watched as the soldier unlocked the door and held it open.

"General Moon, come with me," the guard said in Korean.

The elder Moon had dark circles under his eyes but otherwise appeared to be in good health.

"Tell General Han I refuse," Moon said. "His coup will fail."

Bond moved quickly and silently. He struck the guard from behind, pulled him into the room, and shut the door. General Moon stared at Bond with incredulity.

Bond looked around the room and said, "It's not like the prison I was in."

"How did you get in here?" the general asked.

Bond ignored the question. "General Han is just a puppet. Your son is pulling the strings."

General Moon looked confused. "My son is dead, thanks to you."

Bond relieved the unconscious guard of his gun and

pulled the body out of the way, behind a table. "No. He survived. He's changed his identity—even his face. But he survived."

"You're crazy."

"You'll see who's deranged."

"I have grieved all this time. My son would not let me suffer like that."

"Oh, he's been planning this reunion for some time. Four of your divisions are massed on the border."

Moon's eyes narrowed. "The troops are still loyal to me. I will put an end to this."

Bond considered the situation and then handed the general the guard's gun. "You'd better take this."

The two men stared at each other. Moon had allowed Bond to be tortured, faked a firing squad . . . and now the British spy was placing his trust in him. The general took the gun, still a little puzzled. Finally, he opened the door and walked out, followed by Bond.

20

Icarus Unleashed

The general walked through the plane's custom-made gymnasium on the way to the front of the plane. It was decorated with ancient swords, Korean rugs, and the like, but also with modern equipment—weights, Nautilus machines, swords, and a punching bag. The bust of Colonel Moon sat on a pedestal, just as it had in Moon's old gym in North Korea. The general stopped for a moment to gaze upon the image of his son as he once was.

He continued on and was met by a guard, who escorted him down the stairs to the observation bay. As he entered, everyone in the room looked up and stared, anticipating the scene that was about to occur. Gustav Graves turned from the map of Korea and looked at his father, his emotions held in check.

Graves spoke in Korean. "General. I am sorry you had to be brought here like this."

General Moon studied the bizarre sight, this white man in a North Korean uniform. He couldn't believe what was in front of him. The general turned to the guard who had escorted him and said, "Arrest this man."

The guard made no attempt to move.

Graves continued, "I knew you would find the adjustment hard to make. You . . . don't recognise my voice?"

General Moon replied in English, "I do not know you."

"You've always found it hard to accept me. That made it a little easier to exile myself, hide among the enemy—*become* the enemy. All the time reminding myself what you taught me. 'In war, the victorious strategist only seeks battle after—' "

"—the victory has been won,' " the general said, completing the sentence. Now he truly recognised his son, and he didn't like what he saw.

"You see, Father, I remember my *Art of War*." He moved to the brassard. "And *this* is what guarantees victory."

The general continued to stare at the monster that was his son as Graves donned the gauntlet and visor.

Bond and Jinx quietly approached the guard standing at the top of the stairs and looking down into the observation bay. Jinx pulled a Sykes-Fairbairn combat knife from a sheath strapped to her leg and threw it into the man's back. Bond caught him before he toppled down the stairwell.

"I'll check out the pilot," Jinx whispered.

"Didn't know you could fly," Bond whispered back.

"You know me, full of surprises," she said, winking.

Jinx disappeared and Bond moved to a position behind the angled screen so that he could see and hear everything that was going on in the observation bay.

Graves punched a button on the brassard and said, "Father, watch the rising of your son."

Icarus responded as it orbited in space, maintaining a speed close to that of the earth's rotation. Once again, the satellite rearticulated, pointing its mirrors so that the sun's rays reflected down to Asia.

Miles away in the Demilitarized Zone, a burst of bright light suddenly appeared, sweeping away the darkness of night and bathing the apocalyptic landscape in the rays of a new sun. After a few minutes, the heat haze swirled and the dust whipped up. As the temperature rose, the Icarus vortex began to churn up the earth. Mines detonated. A column of twisting fire rose vertically, feeding on itself and pulling in debris that ignited spontaneously. The fire sprout became unnaturally violent because of all the explosives being sucked into it.

Then the Icarus light started to move across the Demilitarized Zone. The flaming twister danced along at the head, leaving a trail of scorched earth in its wake.

Graves surveyed the distant necklace of explosions and proclaimed, "Icarus will clear the minefield, creating a highway for our troops. If the Americans don't run, Icarus will destroy them. And then? Japan waits like a bug to be squashed. China will welcome us. And the West will shake with fear at the dawn of a new superpower!"

The three generals watched with awe. General Moon felt only horror.

On the southern side of the 38th Parallel, M and Falco watched the destruction on monitors in the operations room. Satellite views of the Demilitarized Zone also displayed the devastation that was slowly making its way towards them.

"My God," M said.

"Looks like our two didn't make it," Falco said. "One suicide mission too many."

General Chandler, who was as stunned as everyone else, turned to Falco. The NSA chief gave him a grave, subtle nod. Chandler picked up the phone and said, "Get me the president."

Falco looked at M and quipped, "World War Three—made in Korea."

M's palms were sweating. She gripped the back of a chair tightly and said, "Don't count Bond out yet."

Several tense minutes passed. No one said another word until General Chandler muttered, "Yes, sir," into the phone and hung it up. He looked at Falco and M and said, "We got the go-ahead."

Falco addressed everyone in the room, "The second that thing crosses the 38th Parallel we hit them with everything we've got."

M's only comment was, "That may not be enough."

Jinx moved into the galley behind the cockpit and could see the pilot and copilot through the half-open door. She weighed her options and was about to act when the copilot suddenly got up and headed in her direction. Jinx leapt up into a shadowy storage area and pressed her hands and feet against opposite walls, suspending herself there. The copilot walked through the galley and went down the stairs without noticing her. Jinx silently lowered herself and continued her mission.

Meanwhile, above the observation bay, Bond made the decision to take out Graves at the first opportunity. He removed the Walther and aimed it at the man through the glass screen. He was ready to squeeze the trigger when General Moon stepped in front of his son, blocking the shot.

"Stop this now," the general said in Korean. "You will lead our people to destruction."

"You were always weak," Graves replied in English, now the son who would not speak in his native tongue. "You can't accept me because you can't accept greatness."

"The Americans will send nuclear warheads."

"And Icarus will swat them from the sky. The sword is also a shield."

The general produced the pistol that Bond had given him and pointed it at Graves's head.

Graves eyed his father with interest. "Would you kill your own son?"

"The son I knew died a long time ago."

But before the general could fire, Graves's hand whipped out fast, grabbing his father's wrist and turning the pistol around.

On the other side of the screen, Bond now had a clear shot at Graves. He moved slightly to get a better angle and aimed—and was jumped from behind by the copilot. Below them, Graves and the general struggled for control of the weapon as the others watched in shock and silence. Without warning, the general's pistol went off directly into his abdomen. General Moon slumped to the floor.

Graves looked at his father with no emotion. "Like father, like son," she said, then he bent down and ripped the general's stars from his uniform. The three other generals watched Graves warily as he attached the insignia to his own uniform.

Suddenly the glass screen above them shattered as Bond and the copilot crashed through, still fighting for the gun. They tumbled to the floor with a thud and the pistol fired, blowing out a pane of glass in the observation window. Someone screamed as the plane instantly depressurised, creating a deafening screech of air whistling through the cabin. Everyone in the observation bay grabbed something to hold on to as loose objects flew like shrapnel through the air and out of the window. Vlad, unable to gain a handhold, was picked up by the force and slammed against the window. As he was violently sucked out of the plane, more panes were shattered, making the hole even bigger.

Bond held on to the instrument panel while Graves clung to the brassard pedestal. General Moon's lifeless body shot through the opening like a puppet and was then followed by the three terrified generals, one by one.

The plane lurched and went into a nosedive.

In the cockpit, the pilot was thrown forward, hitting his head on the instrument panel. Jinx had been knocked to the floor and was still clinging to the cockpit door as the plane began its descent. Fighting the enormous gravitational pull on her body, she struggled to her feet, crawled into the cockpit, and pulled the unconscious pilot from behind the controls. She threw herself into the seat, buckled in, and put on the headset.

"James, you're flying Jinx Airways," she announced.

She struggled with the stick, leaning into it, willing the plane to level out. Only after a tense forty seconds did the Antonov finally respond and pull out of the dive. The altimeter steadied around five-thousand feet.

Back in the U.S. Army bunker, everyone felt the place shake from the tremors of the distant detonating mines. They could hear explosions and the sound of high winds. Robinson checked a monitor and looked at M.

"One thousand yards and closing," he said.

21

Into the Maelstrom

As the plane levelled, Bond and Graves regained their footing and were able to stand. The wind was howling in from the gaping hole in the glass, but the depressurisation had stopped. The two men squared up to each other, waiting to see who would make the first move.

"It seems your friends have bailed," Bond said, indicating the gaping hole.

Graves seemed unconcerned. Snarling, he pressed a switch on the brassard. It powered up with an eerie hum. Bond knew what it meant and backed away. Graves lurched for Bond and zapped him with a huge jolt of electricity. Bond gasped from the pain but managed to drop and roll to escape the current. Graves went after him, holding out the gauntlet-covered arm. He bore down on Bond and struck him again with a charge.

Bond felt this one surge through his spine, and it momentarily paralysed him. Graves kept the thing in place, delivering a massive amount of electricity into Bond's body. Bond's leg kicked out reflexively and landed squarely in Graves's groin. The man yelped and fell back, giving Bond the time he needed to get to his feet and punch him hard in the face.

In the cockpit, Jinx felt strangely alone. She wondered what was going on in the back. Had James survived the depressurisation? Had anyone died? It was too quiet, and this unnerved her. She tried to concentrate on the plane's navigational bearings, but there was damage to some of the instruments. She had no idea which direction they were heading in, but she did know they were flying over the Demilitarized Zone.

Then the darkness outside the plane suddenly disappeared. It was as if the sun had risen in a few seconds' time and was now bright in the sky. Jinx looked in horror and saw that the Antonov was travelling towards the Icarus beam. The vortex of fire spiralled from its base, seeming to beckon for the plane to fly straight into it.

"Damn!" she muttered, and tried to take evasive action. She pulled on the stick, but the plane didn't respond. Jinx leaned forward to get some readings off the instrument panel, and this action saved her life—she saw the reflection of Miranda Frost in one of the screens. The woman had a sword raised above her head, ready to bring it down on Jinx.

Jinx ducked to one side as Miranda struck. The blade just missed her face but managed to slice the mouthpiece off her headset. The sword, an eighteenth-century Chinese *Ken,* imbedded itself in the pilot's chair. In an uncanny display of speed and coordination, Jinx unbuckled her safety belt and "walked" up the instrument panel in front of her in a kind of twisting back flip, pulling another Sykes-Fairbairn knife from its sheath at the same time.

Miranda glared at Jinx and pulled the sword out of the chair. She lunged at her adversary again, but Jinx blocked the attack with the hilt of her knife. Miranda swung the *Ken* horizontally, forcing Jinx to duck and push herself away from the side of the cockpit. The women faced each other with their weapons poised. Jinx could see that Miranda was no amateur with the sword. She handled it with grace, strength, and confidence. Jinx wasn't much of a sword fighter, but she was good with a knife—so good, in fact, that she didn't consider herself at a disadvantage at all.

"Come on, girl, if you think you can do it," Jinx taunted her.

Down below in the observation bay, Bond *was* finding himself at a disadvantage. Graves's gauntlet was a deadly and powerful weapon that was capable of issuing an electric charge from a few feet away. Bond had to work to keep out of its way. The debris in the room, caused by the depressurisation, was not making the job any easier. He had tripped twice on pieces of broken furniture.

Graves moved forward, the brassard glowing ominously. Bond backed up against a panel and spun out of the way just as the jolt blasted the instruments he had been covering just a moment before. But the manoeuvre backfired and Bond lost his balance. Graves had stepped over him and was ready to deliver the finishing blow when a tremendously bright light filled the observation bay. They both looked out the large window and saw that the plane was about to enter the Icarus beam. Bond shielded his eyes.

The Antonov jerked as if it had hit a wall—a wall of heat and turbulence. Everything seemed to just white out, caught in the incredible brightness of the concentrated light.

Graves was caught off guard and had no time to adjust the brassard as the plane was buffeted in the upheaval. He was knocked sideways and into the pedestal that held his marble bust.

The plane's nose was hit hard. The cockpit window imploded, blasting the fighting women through the doorway and down the stairs to the gymnasium. Hot glass showered the area and flames licked the inside of the cockpit.

Jinx was stunned, even though a gym mat had broken her fall. Nevertheless, her body felt as if she had been treated by a mad acupuncturist. She raised herself off the floor and saw that she was covered with tiny cuts and scrapes from the glass. Miranda was in similar condition and was recovering from the impact just a few feet away. They stood, retrieved their weapons, and prepared to continue the bout. Hot wind stormed through the whited-out gym as the walls caught fire. Jinx took a second knife from the collection in the showcase and now had one in each hand. Miranda shrieked and came at her with the sword, but Jinx blocked the attack. Even so, Miranda didn't let up. She kept charging at her opponent, backing her up to a flaming wall. Jinx's shirt caught on fire. Avoiding the swinging sword, she tore off the garment and threw it away. Now dressed in an army T-shirt, she continued to evade Miranda's offensive with agile leaps and feints.

The observation bay was beginning to fall apart. Rivets popped and panels started to peel, revealing the struts of the airframe. Bond and Graves ignored this and continued to struggle with each other, unhampered by the howling hot wind that was blowing through the plane. Bond punched Graves in the stomach, doubling him over; but before he could deliver another blow to the back of Graves's head, his opponent zapped his leg with the gauntlet. The men separated to reclaim ground and breath.

Then the brightness and turbulence ceased as the plane emerged from Icarus' cone. The sudden change in atmosphere prompted them to take stock of their surroundings. Wind coursed through gaping holes in the hull and a fire raged further back in the plane. The aircraft would surely crash in a matter of minutes.

Graves circled Bond, who attempted to keep clear of the arm. "My light is inextinguishable . . ." he said. He got around to a storage locker and opened it with his other hand. Several parachutes were hanging inside. He hooked one over his shoulder and let the others fly out of the gaping hole in the side of the plane. They shot backwards at three hundred miles per hour. "Whereas yours has just blown out."

Jinx and Miranda were unaware that the crippled Antonov, now more skeleton than aircraft, was hurtling unsteadily between the Icarus beam and the vertical firestorm that was still rising from the Demilitarized Zone. As panels peeled off the ceiling, the women moved about the gym equipment, slashing and thrusting their blades at each other. Jinx avoided a powerful swing of the sword by dodging behind the punching bag. Miranda sliced the rope holding it and moved in for the kill. She slashed at Jinx, who ducked, causing the sword to smash against the bust of Graves. The statue broke, surprising Miranda. Jinx used this opportunity to throw one of her knives, but Miranda quickly responded and blocked it with what was left of her sword. Jinx immediately flung the second knife, and this time Miranda, astonishingly, caught the blade with her other hand, millimetres from her chest. She glanced up at Jinx and smiled, but she wasn't expecting Jinx's powerhouse karate kick that followed—slamming the knife into Miranda's heart. Miranda gasped and dropped to the floor, desperately clutching to the life that was slipping away from her. Jinx watched, panting, until the woman ceased to move, then turned to see through the unusable remnants of the melted cockpit.

The maelstrom of fire was only seconds ahead.

Down below, Graves had strapped the parachute on and was moving towards the opening in the hull.

"So good-bye," he said to Bond. "It is your turn to die this time. Life is full of death, James."

But Bond leapt at Graves, who batted him down with another jolt of power from the gauntlet. Graves laughed until he noticed that Bond was holding on to the parachute's rip cord. He felt his heart stop as his chute paid out and was caught in the wind barrelling through the nose of the plane. The chute was sucked up the staircase, carrying Graves with it into the gymnasium. The canopy eventually blew out the hole in the roof where a panel was missing. Graves managed to grab the exposed edge of another panel and hung on for dear life.

Only one bolt was keeping the panel in place and was threatening to tear free.

Bond slowly ascended the stairs and faced Graves. "You were saying something about death?" he asked.

Graves looked ahead and saw the firestorm the plane was about to hit. He stared back at Bond as he understood his fate. Bond reached up and pulled the bolt free. The skin of the plane peeled backwards with Graves still hanging on. He was dragged back along the top of the aircraft, his chute burning up as it flew into the maelstrom, followed by Graves himself. As he was consumed in the flames, the brassard was destroyed and the Icarus light abruptly went out.

22

Another Day of Life

M and Falco watched from the bunker as the fire-storm wavered only a few hundred yards away. Emergency crews had been summoned and were standing by, ready to tackle the onslaught of destruction. Robinson had arranged for immediate evacuation for M and Falco, but they had refused to leave. Robinson was about to go over M's head, to the prime minister, for a direct order to leave when suddenly everything changed.

The roar of the burning soil subsided almost as quickly as it had begun. The swirling hot winds and flames died out, leaving trace fires in the path that the beam had taken. Now there was an eerie silence.

Falco exhaled and M allowed herself a smile at what her man had accomplished.

But although the column of swirling fire and smoke

had weakened a little at the base, it was still violent at five thousand feet. The decrepit skeleton of the Antonov was still flying, even though half of the panels had peeled off and flames raged from its rear. Then, amazingly, the aircraft flew out of the hell cloud.

Bond and Jinx found each other in the gymnasium and hugged.

"The cockpit's shot," she said.

"So are the chutes."

They clung to each other in the jostling wind. The plane creaked horribly as more panels ripped away above them.

"Looks like we're going down together," she said.

Bond remembered something and replied, "No time for that. We've got a helicopter to catch—before it falls."

Her eyes widened with understanding.

They ran for the stairs to the hold, but flames leapt up at them, blocking the way. They looked towards the door at the rear of the gym, but it was on fire as well. Bond eyed the objects in the room and ripped a ceremonial rug from the wall. He threw it over the stairs, temporarily blocking the flames.

"Go!" he shouted. Jinx headed down, but as Bond began to follow, a bloody face loomed out at him.

"James," Miranda said, "take me with you." She looked as if she were at death's door, clutching the wound in her chest.

Bond shook his head. "This is the life you've chosen."

Miranda expected no mercy, but she obviously wanted to delay Bond long enough to thwart his escape. Flames began to eat through the rug on the stairs.

"Don't you want to know why I did it?" she asked.

Bond considered the question but realised that he felt no curiosity whatsoever.

"No," he replied.

He disappeared down into the hold a second before the rug burst into flames. Miranda slumped back, waiting for the inevitable.

Jinx had meanwhile reached the hold and punched the button to open the ramp at the rear of the plane. It groaned like a wounded beast, but the mechanism still worked. A rush of air and smoke overwhelmed her and she could see large flames trailing behind the aircraft.

"James?" she called.

"I'm here!" he shouted, arriving beside the helicopter.

"We got a gridlock," she said, pointing to the two sports cars between the chopper and the ramp.

"Get in," he told her. She pulled the doors to the Hermit open and suddenly a wind gusted back towards them as more panels ripped off the plane. Jinx clambered into the helicopter as Bond struggled to move forward towards the panel that controlled the loading apparatus. He pushed himself, fighting the powerful force, until he was within reach. He slammed the buttons, and with a shriek the loading chain to which all the cargo was attached began to pay out.

Immediately the two cars and the helicopter started to move back towards the ramp. Bond rushed to catch up with the Hermit, but it was sliding much faster than he had anticipated. The weight of the sports cars pulled it harder. The Ferrari dropped off the ramp into the atmosphere, followed quickly by the Lamborghini. Bond raced along and reached for a grip on the helicopter as the coursing wind blasted it backward on its wheeled pallet. He just managed to grasp the edge of the open door and swing inside as the helicopter plunged off the ramp.

The Hermit fell from the plane just as the Antonov finally broke up into hundreds of pieces. The aircraft peeled like a banana, its engines flying off in different directions and flames licking down towards the free-falling helicopter. Burning debris tumbled towards the minefields below.

Bond struggled with the Hermit's controls, willing its engines to start. The helicopter was falling fast, catching up to the two sports cars because of its greater weight.

"I said I was a jinx," she muttered.

"I should have warned you," Bond said, fighting the controls. "My relationships don't last either."

The ground raced towards them and air whistled through the rotors. Behind them in the hold, a large metal container strained against the cargo net securing it. Suddenly the lid broke open and a massive quantity of diamonds spilled out. Jinx looked back and saw them. "At least we're gonna die rich," she said.

Bond continued to flick switches as the Hermit tumbled . . . and then air gripped the rotors and started to turn them. Gradually the rate of fall slowed as the rotors sped up, but the ground was still coming up fast.

"Come on . . . !" Bond shouted.

Jinx clutched his arm, ready to say good-bye.

Finally, a mere hundred feet from impact, the Hermit's engine kicked in. The rotors' momentum was strong enough to allow the helicopter to come right down to the ground and hover within a few feet of it, marginally missing a deadly fate. The Ferrari and Lamborghini were embedded in the ground nearby like two bizarre tombstones.

Bond and Jinx turned to each other, not believing their good fortune.

"You said something about going down together?" he said.

He manipulated the controls and the helicopter zipped away low across the ground.

An atmosphere of relief pervaded the operations room in the bunker. M, however, noticed Falco's characteristic frown return to his face.

"Now what's the matter?" she asked him.

"I hear your man isn't too hot at returning government property," Falco replied.

"You're worried about your Switchblades?"

"Not really. I'm worried about my agent."

M regarded him with a twinkle in her eye and turned to Robinson. "Get Bond back to London as soon as possible," she ordered.

"Yes, ma'am," Robinson said with a smile.

Miss Moneypenny sat at her desk in MI6 headquarters, working after hours again. Typing the reports on the Korean operations had taken longer than she had expected and she wanted to get out of the place before midnight. As she pressed the key to print a document, James Bond walked in, looking fresh and sharp.

"James . . ." she said, smiling.

"Moneypenny . . ." he replied lovingly.

She got up, swept everything off her desk, and pulled him down by his tie. Bond responded and the repressed passion of many years was unleashed in a sweltering embrace. Their passion increased as the kisses came faster and faster . . . until a light flickered and interrupted the scene—

—as Q stepped into his workshop, looking for something, only to find Moneypenny alone in the Virtual Reality Chamber. He looked through the window and saw her writhing with pleasure, her eyes closed and lips pursed.

"Moneypenny?" he called over the loudspeaker.

She shrieked, surprised and embarrassed. She quickly ripped the VR glasses off her head.

"I was just testing it out," she said breathlessly.

Q's pride in his invention replaced his irritation. "Rather hard, isn't it?" he asked, referring to the virtual obstacle course.

"Very."

"How many did you get?"

"Only one unfortunately."

Waves lapped the shoreline with an undulating rhythm that was mesmerising. Birds sang to one another somewhere in the distance and dusk had brought the elusive orange and red colours out of the sky. It was the magic time, the perfect denouement to the drama that had unfolded over the last twenty-four hours.

James Bond and Jinx didn't take the wondrous beauty around them for granted.

They had arrived at a beach northwest of Inchon just in time for sunset, landed the Hermit, climbed out, and fallen onto the sand. After being so close to death, the couple were now determined to reaffirm the joy of being alive. Surrendering to the moment, they kissed passionately as if there were no tomorrow.

Jinx pointed to a lone bamboo beach shack and Bond

nodded wordlessly. An hour later they lay on a straw bed inside the hut, surrounded by the diamonds from the now empty container.

"James? Can't you leave it in there just a little longer?" Jinx asked.

"You know as well as I do this is illegal." He pulled a large diamond from her navel and tossed it into the pile.

"It costs nothing to dream," she said. "Shouldn't we be getting them back?"

"Oh, I think the world can do without us for a few days."

"James," she said, with feeling, and they kissed again.